I0718417

Steal:
Forty Thieves
Retold

DEMELZA CARLTON

A tale in the Romance a Medieval Fairy Tale series

ISBN: 978-1-925799-32-3

DEDICATION

This one is for Sasha Wasley, in thanks for her workshop where Mithra introduced himself to me so clearly I wanted to go home and write his story then and there…

One

"These figures can't be right. Are you sure, Peter? I'm going to check them over again."

Peter pulled the ledger out of Mithra's hands. "Yes, they're correct. Father is going to be delighted. This month has to be the most profitable one he's ever known. War is good for business, contrary to anything those grumbling old men say in Rialto. Father was a wise man to leave his family behind and set up here. I would never have been born, because younger brothers aren't allowed to marry and have children, and you would be forced to take an apprenticeship under your sour old uncle. I bless whatever prophet, false or otherwise, who persuaded the Seljuk army to attack Edessa and leave us here at Dorylaeum as the largest city left trading with Rialto!" He jumped to his feet and spread his arms wide. "This war will make our fortunes, Mithra! And to celebrate, I'm taking you to dinner."

Mithra could not refuse such a generous offer, for while they might be fellow apprentices at present, Peter stood to inherit all of his father's substantial merchant business one day, and Mithra's father was a woodcutter whose most valuable possessions were the three donkeys and a handcart he used to collect firewood every day.

Not for the first time, Mithra wondered why his father had apprenticed him to a successful merchant like Simon, when he'd never have the money to buy trade goods to sell at a profit, like Simon or Mithra's uncle, Kasim.

Unless Mithra married a girl with a large dowry, as Kasim had. But Mithra's heart would not allow him to do something so mercenary. His parents had married for love and Mithra meant to do the same, if the girl of his heart's desire would have him. Speaking of which…

"There she is!" Peter said, gesturing toward the counter.

Cagri blushed prettily at something her customer had said, then tugged at her veil to cover a curl which had escaped. Mithra had a sudden vision of her curls all escaping at once, reaching for him and then twining about him like serpents, before bringing him to her as an offering. One look from her deep, dark eyes would hypnotise him so he felt no need to struggle out of her snare, and he would happily serve her all his days.

It was as though one of the ancient goddesses had been made mortal and forced to hand out bountiful trays of bread to the descendants of her former worshippers.

"Wipe your mouth – you're drooling again!" Peter hissed.

Mithra swiped his sleeve across his face, only to find it dry. He shot a hurt look that only made Peter grin wider.

"I can't blame you. Lechem's bakery has both the sweetest and the most savoury delights in the whole city." At another look from Mithra, Peter added, "I'm only talking about the food. You're the one who thinks Lechem's daughter is sweeter than any pastry. My father has some Rialto lady lined up to marry me, who will likely look elsewhere if she knows I even looked at another woman before I beheld her. To hear Father tell it, Rialto ladies are so jealous they should all wear green!"

Mithra managed a smile, but he didn't feel it. The famed city of Rialto was half a world away, the necessary gateway to trade in the north, but he would never reach it if he married for love, let alone see its ladies. But winning Cagri as his wife would surely be worth it...

"I will miss the food from here. The north does not have the same spices," the man in front of them lamented.

"So take some with you. Some to trade, some to be added to your food, and use your profits from the voyage to buy more when you return!" his companion said.

The first man shook his head. "I fear it will not be safe to return."

"Why not? Has your mind become so addled you're now believing stories about sea monsters? Or the ones about girls who sit beside the northern sea and sing up storms? Sailors' tales, all of them, and not a drop of truth to be found."

"'Tis not imaginary monsters I fear, but stories from the south. Did you not hear? The Seljuk army is headed here next. They mean to drive all Crusaders back into the north, and take their land for their own."

A third man chimed in, "Then we close the gates, and prove why the ancients built a fort here in the first place! Dorylaeum has never been taken by an enemy, and it will not be conquered now! This city has stood for more than two thousand years, and may it stand for two thousand more!"

A ragged cheer went up at these words, but it died away quickly.

The last time two armies had met on the plains outside the city, the Crusaders had beaten the Seljuks, and though more than fifty years had passed, the Seljuks had no intention of forgiving the Crusaders' descendants for it. The stories of atrocities the Crusaders committed when they reached what they called the Holy City – thousands of citizens killed or sold into slavery – were mirrored by the tales of what the Seljuks had done to Edessa. Dorylaeum was a prosperous city where people of various different faiths lived in relative peace. It was this delicate balance that allowed the city to thrive as it did.

"The Crusaders will come, and save the city again," Peter said. "They have undoubtedly heard word of what happened in Edessa, and are building an army to take the city back even as we speak. If both armies meet outside Dorylaeum again, we will be able to cheer them from the walls!"

Cagri's eyes grew wide. "They would truly fight to defend us, right outside the city walls?" Her hands flew to her heart as her eyelashes fluttered. "Oh, I could not bear to watch. I would be far too frightened."

"I'm sure one of our brave defenders on the

walls would be willing to hold your hand, to bolster your courage with his own. Right, Mithra?" Peter dug his elbow painfully into Mithra's ribs.

Mithra opened his mouth, but no sound came out. By all that was holy, she was so beautiful, she stole his very breath away.

"If you were there, I might be able to bear it," Cagri breathed.

But her eyes were on Peter, not Mithra.

A voice behind Mithra shouted, "It's the Seljuks that would save us from the Crusaders! Last time they came, they slaughtered whole cities and ate the babies! What else can you expect from northern barbarians?"

"Crusaders are not cannibals!" Peter burst out. "They are holy knights…"

The argument raged hotly as Mithra took their meal and carried it outside, following Peter and the other shouting men into the street.

Blows were exchanged, but it was not long before the fight broke up, with little more than bruises and a few bloodied knuckles and noses. This was what passed for peace in Dorylaeum, and Mithra could only hope it lasted.

Peter pinched his still-bleeding nose in his handkerchief. "So what are you going to do to prepare for this war?" he asked thickly.

Pray that war would not venture inside the city walls, probably, Mithra thought but did not say. For either army might kill them all.

"Come on, Mithra, this war will make all our fortunes! Maybe even make you enough so that Lechem will come looking for you to beg you to marry his daughter. What will you do to profit from the coming war?" Peter pressed.

Mithra thought for a moment, as he bit into his meat-filled pastry. He suppressed a moan at how good it tasted. With Cagri as his wife, he would eat like a king. But in order to win her, and her father's permission, he would need a plan.

He closed his eyes. "When the armies come, the city will shut the gates. If there is a siege, we will run short of firewood, for no one will dare cross a battlefield to cut wood. So Father and I need to fill our storerooms with all the wood we can, before they arrive."

Peter nodded. "After the battle is won, there

will be funeral pyres, too, don't forget. And both our families should buy good stores of food, before the prices go up, in case there is a siege. If not, we can always sell them as supplies to the soldiers."

"We should take inventory of what food and drink your father has in his warehouses, and whether it can be sold at a higher profit here than shipping it north."

"The Crusaders will want the wine we received last week. I wonder if we'll get another shipment before the army arrives…"

They headed back to Peter's house, discussing plans for the coming war as if it was nothing more than another commercial opportunity. And perhaps it was.

But why did the pastry in Mithra's belly insist on churning like the sea in a storm?

One thing Mithra did know: whoever came to the city, whether Crusaders or Seljuks or both, the coming battle would change his life forever.

Two

The first riders arrived shortly after dawn, and the rest followed like a biblical flood that refused to be stopped. Melisende watched them from the top of the keep, and even when she was called down to dinner, still the river of knights marched through her head, banners flying, proclaiming to heaven itself that they would avenge her.

She longed to march with them.

"Is the meat particularly good today?" Father asked. "Or are your thoughts not on your food at all?"

She blinked, focussing on her almost empty trencher. She could not remember tasting her dinner at all. No matter. "Crusaders must be the most saintly knights in Christendom," Melisende said dreamily.

Her brother simply stared at her. As though it wounded him that she didn't think he was as good as them. Poor Godfrey.

She continued, "I'm surprised you aren't going to join them, now you're a knight, Godfrey. Isn't knighthood all about honour? Travelling so far from home to lay down your very life to save the Holy City...so honourable you cannot help but be named a saint." If Godfrey went, then surely her father would agree to let her go. It was said that a king and queen were leading their people in this crusade. Her father could hardly object to his own daughter going if it was suitable for queens.

But Father frowned. "More like the least saintly. Though I have no doubt Godfrey earned his knighthood with honour, the truth of knighthood is little more than being able to sit upon a horse without falling off, and knowing one end of a sword from the other.

Most of them have only taken up the cross for the glory of it, or the promised pardon of all their sins. They are men who are not heroes at home, or who have no hope of heaven without a good deed so great, it erases everything else they have done. Younger sons and troublemakers – those their fathers would not miss, if they do not return. Unlike my sons, who are very much needed here at home." He signalled for a servant to refill his wine cup. "I am delighted that none of your brothers have decided to join this fool scheme."

Melisende's heart sank. Godfrey was nothing if not an obedient son. Especially after he'd somehow made a mess of trade negotiations in Rialto. No one would tell her the details about what he'd done, but from the whispers she'd heard, it had something to do with someone's daughter. She knew it couldn't have been that bad – knightly Godfrey wouldn't dishonour a lady – but perhaps he'd managed to offend her somehow. Most likely by refusing to kiss or touch her, if the stories she'd heard about Rialto women were true.

"I'm sure my brothers will find plenty of

other foolish things to do instead," Melisende said sweetly.

"Your brothers are not foolish. They might make mistakes occasionally, but none of them are foolish," Father said.

"Then why hasn't Godfrey returned to Rialto, when we all know how much he longs to?" she asked.

From her father's shocked expression, she decided her arrow had struck its mark. Finally, someone would tell her what he'd done.

"Godfrey's trip to Rialto was ill-timed, is all, and the reason he hasn't returned is nothing to do with anything he did. Godfrey knows all too well why this crusade is foolishness from start to finish, as well as what kind of men will form the bulk of that army."

"Stop talking in riddles, Father. I'm no longer a child, and it won't be long before I am old enough to be mistress of my own destiny. What happened?"

"Godfrey, tell her."

But her brother's eyes were down on his food, his thoughts as base as the horses he loved so much. Sometimes she wondered if his mind was addled, he seemed to think so slowly.

"Godfrey!"

Godfrey blinked, finally looking up to meet Father's gaze. "Yes?"

"Tell your sister what the crusading army has done."

Her heart sank again. She didn't care about the Crusaders – she wanted to know about Rialto. And if neither of them was going to tell her…then she did not need to listen to them any more.

When Godfrey finished talking, he excused himself to check on the horses, and Melisende took that as her opportunity to leave, as well.

Yet when she reached the top of the keep, the last of the Crusaders were gone, likely into the valley and the town below.

If she wanted to see them again before they left, she'd have to follow them down, or climb up to St Michael's Spire, the watchtower that stood on the hill between Father's keep and the valley.

Whatever direction she chose, she would definitely need a warm cloak tonight. Which

meant a detour to her chamber to fetch one,
before she had to decide.

15

Three

When Mithra reached home, he found it empty. His father was evidently using the last few hours of daylight to cut as much wood as possible. His was a good example to follow, and Mithra was nothing if not a dutiful son.

Mithra dug out the old handcart that his father had used before he'd become the proud owner of first one, then two, and now three donkeys, all of which were out working with him right now. Mithra might not have time for a full day's work, but he'd probably manage to fill the handcart before it was too dark to see and the guards shut the city gates.

He headed down to the bend in the river, hoping to find some trees washed down by the recent rains. Luck was with him today. The sodden branches cleaved to his axe like willing lovers. Like he hoped Cagri would, when she became his wife.

He couldn't imagine her being anything but eager. She always had such a ready smile, always willing to get whatever a customer wanted. That kind of willingness in a wife, wanting to be bedded whenever he wished…why, it was the kind of happiness a man could only dream of.

Mithra didn't dare dream for long, for dreaming wasn't doing, and he wouldn't have a wife at all until he had the kind of wealth that made wooing a wife a worthwhile pastime. So he hacked and he stacked, until he'd reduced a goodly bunch of branches into a cartload of firewood to sell, once it had dried out. He estimated there was at least another cartload left, but he could return in the morning for that, before he was expected at Simon's shop.

It wasn't a fortune yet, but it was a start,

Mithra told himself as he trudged home with the weight of the handcart trundling along behind him. He'd need a lot more before Father's store rooms were full. He could only hope both armies held off for as long as possible.

Four

Melisende waited until it was dark before stealing down the servants' stairs. The house had been silent for some time, so if she was quick and quiet, no one would be the wiser until morning.

But luck was not with her tonight, for she ran headlong into a solid form headed up the narrow stair.

Between the definitely masculine exclamation and his horsy smell, she knew she'd found no servant.

"Godfrey! What are you doing here?

Looming out of the darkness like that, you nearly made me scream and wake the whole house!" she said.

"I'm going to bed." He eyed her. "Where are you going?"

It was on the tip of her tongue to tell him she was merely going down to the kitchen to fetch something to help her sleep. But not even Godfrey was stupid enough to believe she'd wear a cloak to the kitchen. She could lie and say she'd been summoned to town to help someone, for she was the best healer the town had, but if by some miracle he divined her true purpose for going to town, he would try to stop her.

"If you don't tell me, I'll be forced to tell Father, and he'll send men out to bring you back," Godfrey warned.

"Oh, don't tell Father!" she burst out. She grasped his arm with both hands. "Swear you will not tell Father, and I will tell you."

"Are you meeting a lover?" he demanded.

Trust a man to think of something so silly. As if she would allow one of the boys in town to so much as touch her.

"Swear to me, Godfrey, or I shall tell you nothing."

Long he looked at her, until finally he gave in, as she knew he would. "Very well. I swear I shall not tell Father."

She nodded. "I am going up to St Michael's Spire." There would be little to see in the darkness, so before he could ask why, she added, "To watch the army march out on the morrow." Let him think she would walk up the hill to the watchtower slowly, arriving in time see the dawn. While her other brothers might suspect her talents, she was certain Godfrey did not know about them.

He nodded as if he understood, and she breathed an inward sigh of relief.

"Would you like me to come with you to protect you on the road?" Godfrey asked.

She choked back a laugh. "Of course not. With your big boots clomping along beside me, everyone from the castle to the town will know there's someone on the road alone, ripe for robbing. If I go alone, no one will even know I was there."

He hung his head, and she felt bad for

bringing up his shortcomings. Heaven knew he had a good heart and plenty of courage, even if his wits worked a little slower than most. "As you wish," he said. He headed up the stairs, turning sideways to squeeze past her.

No, she could not let them part so. Though she might change her mind, she would regret this moment if the plan she had begun to form came to fruition.

"Godfrey."

He stopped and turned.

She took a deep breath. "You're a good and honourable knight, but you cannot protect everyone. We both know my fate will take me far from here." To the Holy Land, she wanted to say, but she could not, for he'd surely stop her.

"Safe journey," he said, resuming his ascent.

She smiled in the dark. He only meant to the Spire, not all the way to the Holy Land, but still he wished her well.

"You, too, brother," she said softly as she headed out to meet her fate.

Five

"They're here, they're here!" a small boy shouted as he ran past Simon's shop.

Both Peter's and Mithra's ears pricked up. There was no need to ask who – the whole city had been humming with rumours about how close or far away the Seljuk army were.

"Go and see what the fuss is about," Simon said, shooing the young men out into the street.

"Last to reach the walls has to sweep out the shop!" Peter called over his shoulder as he set off at a run.

Mithra laughed and followed. They wove through crowded streets, dodging other, equally curious citizens, until they reached the wall at practically the same moment. While others queued to get through the gates, Peter pointed at the steps leading up, and led the way to the top of the walls, where several guards stood watching.

No need to ask where the army was coming from, for all eyes were fixed on a distant dust cloud. A cloud that grew larger even as they watched.

"There must be hundreds of them," Peter breathed.

"Thousands," one of the guards corrected.

When finally the shapes of men on horseback emerged from the cloud, Mithra began to believe him. Rank upon rank, they rode out, heading for Dorylaeum, only to stop less than a mile from the gate.

"What are they doing?" Peter asked.

They were milling about by the river, much like the wives waiting outside Lechem's bakery each morning before it opened.

"They're waiting," a guard said.

"For what?"

But no one had an answer, until a man the others appeared to defer to starting waving his arms in a determined fashion and his men moved to where he'd directed them.

"Close the gates!" someone shouted, and the rumble of the gates moving into place thrummed through their feet.

On the plain below, the army didn't move into some sort of attacking formation, as Mithra had expected. Instead, most of the men dismounted and began to make camp.

Peter raced home to tell his father the news, while Mithra stayed to watch. He'd heard tales of the massive fortifications the ancients had constructed when besieging cities, and he had to admit he was curious to see how such things were done.

He stayed standing on the walls until it was too dark to see, but all he saw of the camp were cookfires dotting the plain.

When morning came, it seemed a siege or even some sort of fortification were not part of the army's plan. They'd settled en masse beside the river, with no intention of attacking the city.

Consequently, by the time Mithra reached the city gates with his handcart, they were already open, and he wasn't the only one heading out about his business.

Now he'd cleared the riverbanks, he had to move deeper into the forest to collect firewood, but the wood wasn't as wet, so it was easier to haul the cart home when he was done. The sun was high in the sky by the time he emerged from the woods, and he had to hurry back or risk being late to work.

When he reached Simon's shop, Mithra was surprised to find it wasn't open yet. He'd been apprenticed here for long enough to manage the shop by himself, though, so he opened the doors and pasted what he hoped was a helpful smile on his face, for the streets were full of soldiers and citizens doing brisk business that neither Peter or Simon would want to miss out on.

When the sun set, he closed the shop, and set off for Simon's house to see why no one had come to the bazaar that day. With him, he lugged a clinking bag of the day's takings, which he planned to proudly present to Master Simon as proof that he'd successfully completed his apprenticeship.

Six

Out the side door, following the wall around to the gate until she reached the road, and Melisende was free. Moonlight illuminated her path, setting her cloak aglow. It was a sign, she decided. Definitely a divine one. She was doing the right thing.

Melisende bit her lip, tasting the magic that flowed through her veins, and began to run. Trees and fields flew past, while the road was firm beneath her boots. Her brothers would never know the sheer exhilaration of this kind of speed – not even on Pegasus, Godfrey's favourite horse, at full gallop. Godfrey did not know that she'd raced his horse many a time, and the mare had never won a race. Not that the mare had minded — she'd loved to run almost as much as Melisende.

The road forked ahead, leading down to the town or up to St Michael's Spire. She paused for a moment, looking up. She could ascend the hill and look down on the army from the isolation of the high tower, as she'd said she would, or she could head down into the thick of things, and become part of the wondrous undertaking that was a crusade.

She had stood apart long enough. Melisende turned toward the town, only to find someone running toward her. The girl's panting breaths were louder than the patter of her footsteps on the road.

The girl slowed to a stop, then doubled over to catch her breath. "Lady Melisende? What are you doing here? It is not safe, not with the army encamped just outside town."

It was safe enough when you moved too swiftly to see. Not that Melisende intended to share her secret with one of the village girls.

She knew the voice but…Melisende squinted at the girl's face. "Jella?" she asked.

"Yes," Jella wheezed.

"What are you doing out here without your cloak? You'll freeze, or worse, catch a cold again, and be in bed for a week. How will your father keep up with business in the inn with you lying abed?" Melisende unfastened her own cloak and wrapped it around the girl's shoulders. "There. That should help."

Jella's eyes grew wide, shining in the moonlight. "Oh, no, Lady Melisende, this cloak is far too fine for me. I couldn't…"

Melisende's hand clamped over Jella's frozen fingers, stilling them, before she tied the cloak at the girl's throat. "Return it to the castle when you are done with it, then. I have others." She reached into her bag and drew out a plain brown one that had once belonged to her brothers. They'd all outgrown it, with their broad shoulders, but it fit her just fine. "Now, what are you doing out here? Are you coming up to the castle to fetch me? Is someone sick?"

Jella shook her head. "Father sent me up to the watchtower with a message for Uncle

Beatus. He said to stay up there until the army leaves. They're bad men, my lady. You should not be out here. It isn't safe."

She darted a glance behind her.

Melisende heard it, too.

"Horses. Must be men from the army. Quick, hide, my lady!" Jella ran into the trees beside the road, blundering about until she half-fell into a bush.

Hoofbeats approached, accompanied by bawdy calls from the riders.

No, these were not the kind of men she wanted to meet. These were Crusaders with souls so deeply steeped in sin, they were desperate for redemption. God help the Holy Land if these were the best they could send.

That's where she came in, wasn't it? To lend the army a small mite of virtue, so that this grand undertaking might win. She had no choice but to go with them, no matter what her father said.

Melisende bit her lip and began to run again.

Seven

When Mithra reached the prestigious Crusaders' Quarter where Peter's family lived, the lanterns had been lit and there seemed a lot of people moving about at a time when they were usually enjoying their evening meal. Perhaps it was some sort of Christian holy day that he'd forgotten, Mithra told himself.

But all the people he saw were soldiers, or labourers who lived in the poorer part of town where Mithra and his father lived. A cart stopped outside the house that belonged to Peter's neighbour, a Rialto horse merchant who'd returned to Rialto some time ago, and several labourers started loading chests from the house into the cart.

Maybe the merchant didn't meant to come back, and he'd sent for his things, Mithra thought, until he saw a cart outside Simon's house, too. This cart wasn't empty – it held long, cloth-wrapped bundles like the one being carried out of Simon's door right now. A bundle that looked suspiciously like…

The breeze fluttered the cloth, pulling it away from the horrors it covered. Mithra saw Peter's face, wide eyed and staring, before one of the soldiers pushed the cloth back where it belonged. Peter's body was flung into the cart atop the others, just as another bundle was brought out.

Mithra didn't want to, but he forced himself to step forward to lift the sheet on this body. Simon's face was crusted in blood, barely recognisable, but the man could be no one else.

"Hey! Who are you? Are they your family?" a soldier demanded, drawing his sword to bar Mithra's path.

Mithra shook his head. "I was apprenticed to this man. My father and I live beside the Meat District, behind the markets."

"And who is your father?"

"Ali Baba, younger brother of Kasim, who lives in the Merchants' Quarter." Though more merchants lived here in the Crusaders' Quarter than the Merchants' Quarter, Mithra thought but did not say.

The soldier lifted his eyebrows and sheathed his sword. "You're not apprenticed here any more. The family is dead. Infidels will not be tolerated in this city, and all their goods are forfeit." He waved at the cart full of the horse merchant's things, which had now moved up to Simon's door. Or what had been Simon's door. "If you know of any other infidels in the city, tell us where they are hiding, and you will be rewarded. Anyone who helps them hide will die a traitor's death alongside the infidels."

The breeze seized Peter's shroud, and whipped it away, showing the corpse in all its gore. Peter's tunic was black with blood, except where someone had sawed a hole in his tunic and the belly beneath, spilling out his entrails for the flies to feast on.

Mithra choked back the horrified sound that tried to escape from his throat.

Had it been only yesterday that he and Peter had planned to profit from the arrival of this army? Yet here Peter and his whole family lay dead – good people, for all their faith was different to his own – while he lived. Worse, he'd spent the whole day politely doing business with the men who'd murdered his master.

He'd barely eaten all day, but Mithra managed to stumble into an alley before retching up everything down to a mouthful of bile. It wasn't until he reached up to wipe his mouth that he realised he still carried a bag of Simon's gold.

One day, when the army left and it was safe to travel again, he would take it to Simon's family in Rialto, and tell them what had happened.

Until then, he would keep it safe, for by the time the army's bloody work was done, it would be all that was left of his friend and the family he'd loved almost as dearly as his own.

He felt laugher bubble up in his throat as a horrible thought struck him, but he forced it back down. He, a faithful Muslim of the same faith as the Seljuks, now waited for the Christian Crusaders to arrive, so that he might lay his Christian friend's soul to rest in the way Peter would have wanted. The Crusaders would arrive too late to save Peter's body, but they might help save Mithra's soul.

Eight

Mithra didn't have the heart to go home, for he would have to tell his father about Peter's family's fate, so he wandered the city, with little thought to where he was going until he became aware of his belly complaining of hunger.

He stopped and realised he'd walked all the way to Lechem's bakery, which was currently serving a crowd of people their evening meal. He joined the queue.

Whether it took an age or merely a moment, Mithra did not know, but he found himself standing before the counter. "What would you like?" Cagri asked, her eyes as dull as he felt. Evidently she'd already heard the news.

Mithra ordered a meat pastry – Peter's favourite – and exchanged a few coins for his food.

"I can't believe he's gone," Mithra said.

Cagri blinked. "Who?"

"Peter, of course! We'd come in here together almost every day, and order exactly the same thing. And now…I'll never see him come down from the Crusaders' Quarter, eager to open the shop."

Cagri wrinkled her nose. "What do I care for some Crusader? Probably plotting to kill us all in our beds, the moment he gets the chance! Now, out of the way before I report you as a traitor, too." She shooed him away with a disdainful hand, before her angry expression softened and her eyelashes fluttered. Just like the way she used to look at Peter. "What can I do for you, handsome?" she simpered.

Mithra turned to find two soldiers behind him. His eyes caught on one man's sleeve, darkly spotted with dried blood, as though he'd thrust his sword so hard into his victim that the blood had spattered all the way up his arm.

He could have been the man who killed Peter, or Simon, or any one of the innocent citizens whose bodies had been bundled into shrouds on that cart.

Yet Cagri served them with a smile, as she spat on Peter's memory.

Mithra moved aside, letting the men through, and forced himself to eat the pastry as he watched Cagri with new eyes.

He'd loved her, thought her the sweetest, most beautiful girl he'd ever laid eyes upon, a goddess made flesh.

Now, as he watched her flirt with every man she served, most of them soldiers, he wondered what he could have ever seen in the girl. Her sweet words fell with bitterness on his ears, and he beheld no beauty at all. He avoided her dark zebani eyes that wanted to drink his soul and drag it down to the very depths of torment.

At some point, he must have left the shop, for he found himself wandering the streets again in darkness, tasting bile at the back of his throat, wondering if there would ever be light in the world again.

Nine

Just outside of town, Melisende stopped to change into boys' garb. More castoffs from her brothers that she'd stored in a chest in her chamber, for the boys' clothes fitted no one else now, and the plain tunics and hose were better for sparring than the gowns she wore to please her father.

And herself, on occasion. She had no talent for weaving or spinning or even sewing, but she remembered remedies well enough to take over as mistress of the stillroom when her mother died. So when one of the townsfolk came to seek the ministrations of Lady Melisende, she took care to look like a lady. Herbs and horses had pleased her mother well enough, but Melisende envied her brothers their freedom. They travelled all over Father's lands, and sometimes even further, when a horse was bought or sold.

She'd made Godfrey tell her about everything in Rialto when he'd reached home, until the others tired of his tales, but she never had. She wasn't sure where this crusade would take her, but she hoped she would see some exotic cities on the way.

She fastened her leather breastplate, grateful for its weight against the cold, for the brown cloak was woefully light compared to the thick, white wool one she'd given Jella. But it would be warmer once they reached the Holy Land, or so she'd heard.

Lastly, she took out the leather helm she'd borrowed from the armoury. With the nose and cheek guards, it would hide her hair and her face.

"You won't need it. Most squires are too young to shave, so smooth cheeks aren't much of a giveaway. I would suggest binding your breasts, for the times you're not wearing your aptly named breastplate."

Melisende whirled at the sound of a decidedly masculine drawl.

A man in grey leaned against a tree, a bottle in one hand as though he was about to lift it to his lips for a drink.

"How long have you been there watching me?" Melisende demanded, feeling her cheeks redden. Long enough to see her undress, she was certain.

"Since you arrived and woke me," the man returned, gesturing toward his bedroll and the remains of a fire.

Now she felt even more embarrassed than ever. "My apologies, sir, for I did not see you."

He waved her words away, as if they were nothing. "No knights here, and for that I am grateful. They're a boorish bunch, for the most part. Best stay away from them. For all their talk of honour, they could not watch a maiden undress without wanting to help her, and exact their own high price for the service."

Melisende frowned. "That does not sound

honourable at all to me."

The grey man clapped his hands. "Precisely! So if you wish to keep your honour, or at least hold it a little longer, best keep close to the lover you're playing squire to."

Melisende's mouth dropped open in horror. First her brother, now this man. "I do not have a lover! I am a maiden!"

The grey man did not seem ruffled or even surprised by her outburst. "For now, perhaps, but you cannot think you are the first girl to follow a man into battle. A mistake, in most cases, for if the man had a good squire who fastened his armour properly for him, he'd last longer in battle than most. Yet you're not unfamiliar with armour, so maybe your man might survive. Not to mention the magic you might use to save him."

She'd known the man for barely a moment, and he already knew all her secrets. "What makes you say I have magic?"

A smile touched his lips. "The magic in your blood speaks to the magic in mine. The women in my family are all powerful enchantresses, and you don't grow up around that kind of power without learning to recognise it. Of course, when you appeared in my clearing without casting a portal, I knew there was magic at work, but the bite marks on your lip make it clear that you are a witch." His smile widened. "Or that your lover is a brave man."

She stamped her foot. "For the second time, I do not have a lover! I have no desire to follow some stupid man to war!"

"So why are you here?"

She considered not answering. Lying, perhaps. But in the end, it was the truth that spilled from lips. "Everyone seems so certain the men on this crusade have no honour or virtue to speak of. Without that, how can a crusade succeed? But I recall a tale I heard in church, of a town that was razed to the ground for lack of a virtuous man. If there'd been but one pure person present, the city might have been saved. I'd hoped to persuade my brother to come, but he obeys my father in all things, so he stayed home. And I thought…perhaps it does not have to be a virtuous man at all. Perhaps I could be that one…" She trailed off, suddenly feeling silly. One girl would never be enough to save a city.

But the man only nodded. "Perhaps. One man, or one girl, might make a difference. Or it could be that history is written by the victors, and the people who destroyed that city merely said that the city was full of sinners, instead of simply…other people. As good or bad as anyone else. And the truth is whatever those who survive to tell the tale write after they are done killing." Melancholy shadowed his expression, as he cast his eyes down under the weight of what Melisende could only guess was a terrible memory.

She took a deep breath. "I mean to survive. To return home, where I will tell a tale that is true."

"If that is so, then you will need to be careful. Stay away from those who might do you harm, and when battle is eventually joined, do not stand and fight. Killing leaves a terrible taint on your soul, a stain that you can never wash away. Instead, run. As far and as fast as you can, to a place where you may watch the battle but stay out of sight."

"What honour is there in cowardice?"

"There is very little left of honour in the last moments of life on a battlefield. Especially if you're on the losing side." The grey man gave her a dark look. "It's not too late to head back home."

But it was. She'd made up her mind, and would not turn back now. Melisende shook her head firmly. "I believe my fate lies far from here, and I must go. I can't explain how I know, but…" She shrugged.

"Perhaps your magic makes you a seer of sorts. My mother has always seen the future, and I've never seen one of her predictions to be wrong. Stay or go, 'tis all the same to me. Best stay close to me if you want to live long enough to make it home, though."

Naïve she might be, but she was not as stupid as that. "Why should I trust you? You've already said there's no honour in this army. That means you, too!"

He bowed his head, acknowledging her taunt without taking offence, as her brothers certainly would. "Ah, but I am not a soldier in this army. I merely march with them."

His response only begged more questions, instead of answers. "So you're not a knight, and not a soldier," Melisende said slowly, feeling her thoughts flow as sluggishly as Godfrey's. "What are you?"

"I am a man, much like any other." The answer was too smooth, too practised to be anything other than more evasion.

"But why are you travelling with these men? What is your destination? For you must have one in mind," she persisted.

He eyed her. "Curiosity is the failing of young boys, and of women no matter what their age, yet I will satisfy you, just this once. But I will tell you now, that you will not like the answer." He waited a moment, then went on: "My destination matters not, much like most of these men. I am an assassin on a mission, and once the deed is done, I shall depart."

Melisende took a step back, then another. "You kill people for money!"

He shrugged. "Better than raping, tormenting and then killing them for the sheer fun of it, like most of the others here. The only people who die by my hand deserve it, and if I get paid to deliver justice, where is the harm in that?"

"I'd be mad to trust you!"

"No, you'd be surprisingly sensible. Only a sloppy assassin kills more than they must. As you are not my target, you are perfectly safe with me." He lowered his voice. "Or have you heard rumours saying otherwise?"

Melisende shook her head. "How could I have heard anything about you or any other assassin? I don't even know your name!"

"Ah!" He executed a sweeping bow that wouldn't have been out of place in a royal court. "Zoticus the assassin, at your service." He straightened and grinned. "Should you have need of my services, and the gold to afford them."

She blinked. It was growing lighter, for she could see his face now, as well as the fine wool tunic he wore. He might not be a knight, but he had the manners of a courtier and the clothes of a nobleman. If he truly was an assassin as he said, he could move within the highest circles, and likely held kings and prices in his clientele. Or in his list of victims…

Melisende shivered, then remembered herself. She attempted to drop a curtsey, forgetting she wasn't wearing a gown, and spread the hem of her cloak wide instead. "I am – "

"Don't tell me, or I might call you by name. Especially if you curtsey like no squire ever. Boys bow, and most knights don't bother to learn their squires' names, anyhow, so if you plan to join this benighted crusade, expect to be called Boy or Squire."

She nodded. "All right."

The sound of hooves on the road had her racing to hide behind a tree. She peeped out, cursed, then flattened herself against the trunk.

"So you're not following a lover, but running away from one?" Zoticus asked.

"That's not my lover. He's my brother!" she hissed.

Zoticus grinned. "Oh, then I really must meet this man."

Melisende shot him a dirty look, then bit her lip and bolted.

Ten

Dawn found Mithra at his favourite bath house — favourite because it was formed over a natural hot spring that bubbled up from the earth, and so ancient no one could remember who'd constructed the building that housed it, so the caretaker charged men nothing for bathing in the waters, collecting coin only from those who wanted towels or soap or other services. Mithra usually brought things from home, but no amount of scrubbing could make him feel clean today. Perhaps he should use a couple of hard-won coins to buy some of the bath house soap, to see if it could do any better.

"It's a woman, isn't it?"

Mithra looked up to meet the eyes of a man with a broom. The caretaker, he presumed.

It was everything, he wanted to say, and a woman was both the smallest and worst part of all of it. But the words seemed to stick in his throat.

"Women are the greatest joy and the greatest trouble in a man's life. Your woman's causing you trouble, I think."

Mithra swallowed. "She's not mine. She'll never be mine." Saying the words aloud ripped his heart open anew. How could he have been so wrong about her…

"I'll wager it's because you never tried the thousand and one ways of pleasuring a woman on her. If you'd tried those, she might not have left you." The man raised his eyebrows.

Mithra didn't know what to say. The thousand and one…what?

The man smiled knowingly. "Men are simple, but women…trying to understand them is like trying to catch water with your fingers. They even trouble me, and I'm a eunuch. The things I saw when I was a harem guard..." He shook his head.

Curiosity burned through Mithra's lethargy. His mind simply could not fathom how the man's...no, the eunuch's words could be true. "What is a palace eunuch doing in a lowly bath house?"

The man's smile widened. "Teaching men like you about the thousand and one ways so next time you woo a woman, you will surely win her."

"How much will it cost?" Mithra asked.

The eunuch laughed. "Oh, women pay me well for such knowledge. Gold, jewels, more than a simple man like me needs. How do you think I came to own this bath house? I have no sons, but it seems fitting to share my knowledge with those who might use it. After all, I am but one man, and I cannot serve all the women of the city. A young man like you will catch another wife easily enough, I am sure, and if my words help you win her, then you may pay me whatever price you see fit."

Mithra nodded. It was a wager of sorts. It

seemed fair. "Go on."

"There's a reason women cover their bodies, and it isn't modesty. It's because the slightest touch, when done right, can provoke pleasure such as you have only dreamed of…"

Mithra let the eunuch's words wash over him, as he began to wake properly from his torpor.

Yes, he'd lost his best friend, his job, his master, and the girl he thought he'd loved all in the same day. But he still had his father, and Simon's shop, along with the vow he'd sworn.

Mithra would keep working in the shop as long as the soldiers allowed it, or until all of Simon's goods were gone. In the mornings and evenings, he'd collect wood, and use the coin to pay for his passage to Rialto when the army left and it was safe to travel north again.

And when he was done, then perhaps he'd look for a girl who might be willing to be his wife, and try out perhaps a few of the eunuch's thousand and one ways with her. He would have to return to this bath house, however, to hear the eunuch tell them all, until he managed to memorise them, for he suspected he'd missed a few and the man was already detailing the tenth…

Mithra lay back in the hot water. Now he had a plan and perhaps a future. He owed it to Peter's memory to make good use of both.

Eleven

The sun was high in the sky when Melisende dared to return to the clearing. She found Zoticus preparing a midday meal in his stewpot over a small fire, but no sign of Godfrey.

"Did you tell him about me?" she asked.

Zoticus glanced at her, then turned his attention back to stirring the stewpot. "We spoke about a number of things, but you'll be surprised to hear you didn't come up in the conversation at all."

That wasn't possible. Godfrey must have

come looking for her.

"You're lying," she concluded. "Either he asked about me, or you didn't talk at all."

Any normal man should have been offended, but Zoticus didn't seem to care about her accusation. "Or your brother had more important things on his mind. A girl had been murdered, and he came looking for the culprit, or culprits, as is likely the case. I hinted that I might be willing to hunt them down for him, for a price, of course, but he insisted upon bringing the men to justice himself. A pity. He appears to be that very rare creature, an honourable knight. Yet one who holds justice above his own honour. I told him the names of those he sought, and he rode on. I imagine he will see his mission is futile, and come back presently to offer me the job." Zoticus grinned. "Perhaps he is even now finding courage in the bottom of a tankard in the tavern. For a man's first time hiring an assassin can be as nerve-wracking as one's first kill, or so it seems to me."

"Godfrey does not lack for courage. He is not as bright as some men, but he is steady and loyal and stubborn. If he means to bring a murderer to justice, he will do everything in his power to bring it about." In her hurry to defend her brother, she'd forgotten the most important piece of news. "Did he tell you the name of the girl?"

Zoticus lifted his spoon from the pot and sipped delicately from it. "He did not. Perhaps he did not know it. After all, you are not the only girl who rides with this army." He glanced up at her. "Oh, and in case you weren't aware, it's usually a squire's job to cook the meals."

It was Melisende's turn to smile. "Oh, but I'm not really a squire, and you're not a knight. Besides, the only cooking I'm good at is what I do in the stillroom, and there's no need to make medicine taste nice. So if you want a savoury stew worth sipping from the spoon, best cook it yourself, sir."

Zoticus's eyes fairly sparkled at this. "Well, now," he drawled. "A healer is worth their weight in gold in an army like this one. Not to mention invaluable to a man in my trade." He filled two bowls and set one before Melisende. "Tell me what you know of poisons."

She picked up her bowl and sniffed at it with apprehension. The stew did not smell anything but savoury and appetising, but she knew there were poisons that her nose could not detect.

"There are many substances in the world which may heal in small quantities, but kill if the dose is too large," she began. "And others which may bring about a swift death where a healer can offer no other help." Heaven help her, but the stew smelled so good, and she had not eaten all day.

"What's wrong? Not fine enough fare for your ladyship?" Zoticus asked, looking from the untouched bowl to her.

Melisende swallowed. "I'm not a courtier. I like plain fare just fine. It's poison I do not care to consume."

He burst out laughing. "You think I poisoned the food? Oh, you are a suspicious one, Squire! No, upon my honour, you are safe with me and my cooking. I've rarely used poison, though I might need to in the future. I prefer a blade, slipped between a man's ribs or better yet, sliced across his throat , so that he may see the face of his killer, and the last thing he hears is what crime he has committed for which his life is forfeit. When you're as good an assassin as I am, you may choose which missions you take. May I never stoop so low as to murder a maiden whose only crime is her own naiveté." He raised his bottle in the air, as if in a toast, and drank deeply from it.

Melisende dipped her finger in the stew and licked it. It didn't taste poisoned. "If you're lying, then I shall haunt you from the moment I die to your very last breath," she threatened. Then she began to eat in earnest.

Zoticus only smiled.

Twelve

When the army were done with the houses in the former Crusaders' Quarter, they raided the warehouses. Mithra had already transferred everything he could to the shop in the bazaar, but he wasn't able to save it all.

At least the stock he had saved, he sold at a tidy profit to soldiers, mostly. The luxury foodstuffs he and Peter had saved for a siege found their way into the camp outside the gates at far higher prices than Simon's customers in Rialto might have paid.

Last to sell were the northern furs, brought

from creatures that knew nothing but snow, that soldiers bought as gifts for their wives back home. What their wives wanted with such stuff, he had no idea, but Mithra was not of a mind to quarrel with men who handed over gold by the handful, boasting that the money was their share of the treasure looted from Crusader houses.

Money which he took home every night and locked in the chest that was now all that stood in his father's store rooms, for the wood he'd collected for the siege he'd managed to sell to the soldiers building funeral pyres for Crusader corpses. A thousand times he'd opened his mouth to tell the soldiers that the men they'd killed were no more Crusaders than he was, and that they'd just been ordinary merchants going about their business before they were murdered. Yet he'd closed his mouth again, all those words unsaid, knowing he would only join the bodies on the pyre for supposedly sympathising with Crusaders.

He wished he had the courage to tell the world that he sympathised more with Peter and Simon than he did with the soldiers camped outside his city, but he didn't want to die. Perhaps that made him a coward, someone the soldiers should look down upon, but even as he closed up the empty shop for the last time, he knew the soldiers would soon look down upon him any way.

A merchant and shopkeeper they would at least pay attention to, but a lowly woodcutter was beneath their notice.

As he saw, once again, when he deposited the last of Simon's gold in the chest, and dragged his handcart out of the house to collect more wood.

On the morrow, he would cut wood all day, carting it back to town, before going back out for more, much like his father did. Every day, he would do the same, until the army left and he could journey to Rialto.

And once his quest was complete, he would return to Dorylaeum, never to leave here again.

He was a woodcutter. He'd been born a woodcutter, and, but for a brief time when he'd been an apprentice who dreamed of becoming a successful merchant, he'd live and die a woodcutter. Just like his father.

Thirteen

By the time Melisende reached Byzas, she was sick of walking, sick of sleeping outside and heartily sick of the smell of sweaty, unwashed men. But when she saw that enormous, sprawling city spread out before her for the first time, she found she regretted nothing.

"It's beautiful," she breathed.

"Yes, like the sun making rainbows in the scum atop a cesspool," Zoticus replied. "I could make my fortune here among the royalty and nobility, who are all so worried the others will stab them in the back they don't trust their own families, and rightly so. Everyone else is probably busy quaking in their boots at the sight of an army this big, but the royals are too satisfied with their own superiority to see Crusaders as a threat. If they were ever to close their gates to a Crusader army…that would be an interesting day."

"But aren't they Christians too?" she asked.

"Yes, but of a different sort. They do not show the same reverence to saints. This city is the last crumbling bastion of a dying empire, built by the ancients, but they are too busy squabbling to see it."

"It looks plenty prosperous to me. Look at those palaces!"

Zoticus did not smile. "They are as opulent inside as out, I promise you. Best not to look too closely at them, for the prisons here are barbarous places, where men are locked up for words and looks as much as their deeds."

She'd learned during the journey that while Zoticus might speak in riddles much of the time, he was both observant and knowledgeable about the lands they travelled through. So if he knew about the prison here…

"How did you escape?" she whispered.

"The position of prison guard is not well paid, and men are constantly needed to fill their ranks. So when I took a contract to kill a prisoner before he could be interrogated by one of the resident torturers, it was the easiest job of my career. The man begged for my blade, eagerly snatching it out of my hand to end his own life. When I left the prison's employ a week later, no one was the wiser as to how the man got his hands on a dagger. Most believed he had hidden it upon his person when he was arrested. After that, they searched the prisoners better, I believe."

That wasn't what she'd expected. "They torture people here? How barbaric!"

Zoticus's lips lifted in one of his enigmatic smiles that she knew signified he thought her too naïve to hear any more on the subject, so he would tell her no more.

They passed through the gates in silence. More than once, she had to hurry to catch up to him in the maze of city streets, because she'd been caught staring at yet another building that shimmered in the sun. She had no idea that houses could be so huge.

"I usually stay at the inn near the street of bakers. Cheap rooms, and if I do not like the breakfast, there is plenty to choose from nearby," Zoticus said, gesturing toward a building that looked much older than the ones alongside it. "You should use the time we have here to buy whatever new clothes and weapons you need, and some food for the journey. As much as you think you can carry."

Which wasn't much. Not for the first time, she wished she'd brought a horse and saddlebags full of everything she'd need for her journey. Perhaps she'd have enough coin to buy a packhorse, or at least a sturdy pony. She knew the kind of prices her father commanded for his horses, but she wasn't after a mount fit for a king.

A quick trip to the nearest stable had her wondering if her father was charging too little. A tired-looking donkey that was definitely lame was apparently worth its meagre weight in gold, or so the stablemaster said. He would not part with it for a penny less than her father charged for a well-trained gelding, though it would likely end up in some soldier's stewpot before the week was out.

No horse for her, then, Melisende resolved, taking her time at the blacksmith's instead. A serviceable short sword with no embellishment save the maker's mark cost much the same as one from the smithy at home, though she'd had to wait for the smith to finish re-shoeing a couple of horses before she could make her purchase.

Spare tunics and hose made from a particularly thin kind of linen cost her little, but a good pair of boots small enough for her feet proved impossible to find. There were pretty shoes aplenty, suitable for court or sitting in a chamber, sewing, but for walking halfway around the world, she'd have to wear the boots she'd left home in. At least they were sturdy, for her time running at home stood her in good stead now for all the endless walking. It was a pity she could not run all the way to the Holy Land, but if she arrived alone, without an army at her back, there was little she could do to save anyone.

Besides, she'd missed dinner, and the smell wafting down the bakers' street was trying to steal her attention.

She took her purchases up to the room Zoticus had arranged, took advantage of his absence to wash thoroughly before donning some of her new clothes, and headed out in search of sustenance.

Melisende found the source of the smell was a shop which sold parcels made from thin bread, wrapped around a dark filling that smelled strongly of fish. Yet when she bit into hers, she discovered that the filling consisted entirely of beans, mixed with a spiced sauce that a fish had once swum through, leaving little of its presence but the pungent smell.

She slipped into the shade of an alley to eat her meal, for the road was both hot and busy, only to wish she'd brought something to drink, for the sauce was surprisingly salty. Deciding she could afford to buy a jug of the local wine, she stepped out onto the street before she stopped dead.

Melisende backed into her alley once more, hoping the shadows would hide her while she stared.

It couldn't be Godfrey. It couldn't be.

Yet no other man could possibly ride Pegasus. The only time Father let the mare leave their lands was with Godfrey, who had claimed the horse for his own.

What was he doing here?

Hunting for her, she was sure of it.

Well, she would not let him find her.

She stuffed the remainder of her dinner into her mouth, and set off at a run. She didn't slow until she reached her room at the inn, where she stayed until Zoticus returned.

"You look like you've encountered a ghost," Zoticus said. "You should know that shades rarely cause trouble, and even when they do, they are more intent on avenging their own death than menacing maidens. In the meantime, I have a jug of the local wine that I know will lift your spirits." He brandished the jug in triumph.

Melisende shook her head. "It's my brother. He's here."

"Yes, I thought I'd seen him on the march. I've tried to discourage him as much as I could, small setbacks and the like, but nothing seems to daunt the man, so he has made it all the way to Byzas without turning back. A surprisingly tenacious knight, is Sir Godfrey. I don't see why you don't choose to travel with him instead of my humble self. After all, he has the most magnificent horse, which can carry you and all your clothes, all the way to the Holy Land!"

"If he sees me, he'll only drag me home again. Please, Zoticus. It's only a matter of time before he knows I am here. I'm surprised he hasn't seen me already. Is there nothing you can do that will persuade him to head home without me? I can pay you." Melisende reached for her coin purse.

Zoticus held up his hand. "Now you insult me. I accept payment for assassinations, not for small favours performed for friends. If it is so important to you, I shall stick as close to your brother as his own shadow, until I am certain he has abandoned this crusade."

Only then did Melisende dare to breathe again. "I would be eternally in your debt."

He waved her gratitude away. "Not for

eternity. Just until you performed a suitable favour for me in return. After all, friends help each other, do we not?"

She nodded readily, and he left.

It wasn't until later that she began to wonder what sort of favour the assassin might ask for. Then she began to worry. But Zoticus did not return that night, or the next, as apprehension curdled in her stomach. She wasn't sure what would be worse – to go home in disgrace with Godfrey, or assisting the assassin in his work.

And she dreaded finding out.

Fourteen

Some days, Mithra worked alongside his father, cutting a day's worth of wood before loading it onto his handcart to carry back to town. Sometimes it took him two or three trips, compared to only one for his father with his patient donkeys, and by the time he returned from town, his father had moved on, deeper into the forest to cut wood. Then, Mithra would work alone, cutting and lifting and carrying, until it was too dark to see, and the day's work was done.

At least once a day, he took care to make

sure his path led him close to the army camp, where some of the soldiers were only too happy to buy firewood from him instead of collecting it for themselves. It saved him a trip to town, and firewood fetched a high price here.

Until one morning, when he found the camp in disarray. The Seljuk army were soon to be on the move again. He stopped to ask one of the men he'd become familiar with, "Are you leaving already? Are the Crusaders coming?" He tried to sound concerned, instead of hopeful that opportunity had come at last.

The soldier shrugged. "I have not seen them, if the Crusaders care to come at all," he said. "But the General has slaves to sell, and he wishes to take them to market while the girls still retain their good looks." He jerked his head toward the middle of the camp.

What the camp had previously hidden, now became clear. A fenced-off enclosure, similar to the one that held the soldiers' horses, sat in the centre of camp. Inside its walls were not beasts of burden, but the women and children Mithra thought had died alongside their menfolk in the Crusaders' Quarter. Perhaps even Peter's mother and sisters. Mithra craned his neck for a better look.

As if to oblige him, several of the soldiers opened the gate, and started herding the poor people into a column that would march between two lines of soldiers. Mithra looked and looked, but he could not discern Peter's family from the woeful women wearing little more than rags, which showed the bruises from their ill-treatment all too well.

Mithra wanted to weep. The guards of the city should have protected these people, instead of letting the soldiers steal them and turn them into slaves. He wanted to rage at the army, to fight them all to free the people he knew did not deserve this. But one man was no match for an army – least of all him. He forced himself to harden his heart. Not to their suffering, which smote him to his very soul, but to this soldier and all his fellows, for what they had done.

When the Crusaders came, he would throw open the gates and welcome them, watching with glee as they cut this despicable army to pieces. He hoped they all met the same fate as Peter and his family.

It wasn't until Mithra reached the shelter of the forest that he allowed his anger to surface. His axe was the instrument of his wrath, and the trees his hapless victims. He worked until darkness fell and his arms were too tired to lift the axe that felt almost as heavy as his heart, but still his anger burned.

Fifteen

"You'd best be up and about if you hope to break your fast before we are on the march again," Zoticus said with a brightness that Melisende definitely did not share. Surely it was too early for cheerfulness of any kind, especially from a man who had been following her brother for days on end without sleep, or so it seemed.

Melisende rose. She was gratified to see Zoticus turned his back so that she might dress with some degree of modesty. "Where is my brother?" she asked.

"Oh, I do not think he feels like marching today, or for some days yet. You have no need to worry about him any more."

Dread closed a cold hand around her heart. "He's not...dead, is he?" She knew death meant little to the assassin, but Godfrey was her brother. He didn't deserve to die for simply doing his duty in coming after her, to try and fetch her home.

Zoticus laughed. "No, though he might wish he were when he wakes. He met with a misadventure in an alley last night, and will sleep for some hours yet. When he wakes, I am sure he will wish for nothing more than to be at home in his bed, and likely do everything within his power to make his way there. Of course, once I have done his job for him, meting out justice for this girl he is so determined to avenge, perhaps I shall stop by your father's house to collect a fee for my services. We shall see."

"But he has Pegasus, the swiftest horse alive. This army marches so slowly, he could outpace us in less than a day. You do not know him. He will not stop until justice is served. His honour demands that."

Zoticus sounded thoughtful. "Then it seems I will have to see that someone steals his horse. An easy matter, with a beast so magnificent. I have just the man in mind. Better yet, once we are far enough away from here, I shall simply steal the horse back, and return him to your brother when I come to visit."

Melisende could not help but shake her head. To an assassin like Zoticus, the world seemed so simple. To her, it grew more and more complicated, the further she got from home. Yet today she had no desire to turn back.

Washed, dressed and ready, she headed downstairs with her belongings in a sack over her shoulder, prepared to break her fast and be on her way.

Sixteen

The day the Crusader army arrived was delivery day for Mithra. Both he and his father went house to house, delivering the week's firewood to the clients who his father had supplied for as long as Mithra could remember. His father took the far side of town, while Mithra made trips between the nearer houses and his own with his handcart.

"The Crusaders have come!"

"The Seljuks have returned!"

"They've come to save us!"

"They mean to murder us in our beds!"

"They seek to avenge their countrymen!"

"Close the gates!"

"Open them!"

"Go home and bar your doors!"

"Grab what weapons you can and fight to defend our city!"

Confusion reigned in the city, and Mithra had no idea what to believe when he was hemmed in on all sides by houses and people on the busy street.

If he could but see them with his own eyes, then it would be clear. Mithra dropped his barrow, and began to run. Not since the day he had matched Peter stride for stride had he ascended the walls so fast. Maybe not even then. Because whatever happened today, his fate was tied up in this army's arrival. Whoever they were and whatever they meant to do, his destiny rode beside them.

Yet when he reached the walls, his own confusion was complete. Oh, he could see the approaching dust cloud, coming from the opposite direction to before. He could vaguely discern the outlines of horses and men, headed for the city. But their purpose or religion he could not determine, and the guards were no help.

Just like the people in the city below, they called the approaching army Crusaders or Seljuks, and bellowed for the gate to be both opened and closed.

By the time anyone knew for sure, the army would be upon them.

Mithra stared at the empty plain, where no trace of the former Seljuk camp now stood. He and the other townspeople had picked it clean, hoping that would scour away their memory of war. Now it seemed the initial slaughter of their citizens was only the beginning.

If Peter's death was the beginning, Mithra did not want to imagine the end. Dorylaeum would be destroyed, he was certain of it.

What could one lowly woodcutter do?

Nothing.

So Mithra stayed where he was, took a deep breath, and allowed himself to think for a moment.

If what he saw was the Seljuk army returning, they could only be hurrying to reach the battleground of their choosing before the

Crusaders arrived. That meant the Crusaders were close.

If the Crusaders arrived first, then surely they meant to take the city, or at least make camp outside it. They would avenge Peter, his family, and all the other Christians who had been killed. When the Seljuks heard of their approach, they would return to the city, and battle would ensue.

One way or another, Mithra's wait would be over.

It took an hour or more before Mithra had the answers he sought. The approaching army were definitely Crusaders, and the herald they'd sent ahead shouted to all who could hear him that the Crusaders would defend their faith and avenge their fallen, for they had sworn a terrible oath and so it must be.

Guards bellowed for the gates to be closed, just as a messenger arrived from the other side of the city, conveying orders from the approaching Seljuk army that the city gates should be shut, as they would not permit a single infidel to pass through those hallowed portals to take shelter with any traitor who remained inside. The Seljuks swore they would defend the city against the infidels, even if it meant laying down their lives, for the Crusaders could not be allowed to kill any more innocents.

Once again, Mithra found himself staring at the bare plain, which was about to become home to not one, but two vast armies. In the city below, he heard panicked cries urging people to bar their doors and pray.

Mithra did neither. He intended to stand on the wall and witness the start of a war he feared no one could win. Whatever the outcome, if he survived the day, he knew his life would be forever changed.

So it was with wide eyes and a heavy heart he watched as two armies, two faiths, and two deep desires for vengeance warred for supremacy on the plain below.

Then the two armies collided and the calm plain erupted into chaos.

Seventeen

On top of a hill in the distance, Melisende glimpsed a city surrounded by high walls. "Is that the Holy City?" she asked.

Zoticus laughed. "No, though it's probably just as old. The ancients built it because of the hot springs beneath the ground, and it became a trading centre. They called it Dorylaeum, and it still goes by that name now."

Melisende couldn't help but stare. It wasn't as big as Byzas, but it was still bigger than anything she'd seen before starting this journey. The high stone walls surrounding it made her father's castle look like a child's fort.

She was fortunate to be travelling in the vanguard today, instead of somewhere in the dusty middle of the column. Zoticus had insisted on travelling with one of the small companies led by knights, instead of one of the larger forces commanded by some foreign king. His strategy seemed to have worked, for the knights paid her and Zoticus little to no attention, even when she walked close enough to them to discern the family crest each wore on his breast. They were not brothers, though they appeared as close as family. She knew them by their crests - the raven, the owl, the bear and the horn.

Some days they rode with their men, but others, like today, they kept close together, muttering about their superiors or laughing over some sport they'd engaged in the night before. Today, they were arguing about something, with much emphatic nodding and arm waving to illustrate their points.

Melisende crept closer in the hope of hearing what they were talking about.

"Once we reach the city, there will be sport

aplenty. Why else did I offer our services as scouts? So we might serve in the vanguard today, and have first pick of the city's women," the Bear Knight boasted.

The Raven Knight hunched in his saddle. "I'd sooner have slept between a pair of camp followers than scouting. Damned desert. The days are hot, but the nights are far too cold!"

The Horn Knight offered little more than his loud agreement, as he took a long draught from a wineskin.

"If we'd found a small town or even a roadside inn, you'd all be perfectly satisfied with your scouting mission, having dipped your wick in whatever we found. Who'd have known there'd be no villages along the way?" the Owl Knight said. "If we had, we'd have scouted all the way up to the city, and we'd be safe inside, waiting for the others to catch up."

Melisende smothered the sound of disgust wanting to well up within her. These knights were so base, they considered the success of the crusade to be in the number of women they'd bedded. She'd love to see one of them lose a fight to a proper knight, the sort who protected his lady and fought for her honour. If Godfrey were a better swordsman, she might have wished to have him along to teach these men a much-needed lesson, but it was not to be. If only her own sword skills were better, she'd be willing to take them all on, and show them that a woman was not to be messed with. Perhaps…

"Something is wrong," Zoticus said urgently. He pointed. "The city gates are closed. Dorylaeum is a trading city, where Crusaders and pilgrims have stopped for supplies for more than half a century. Many Christians stayed after the first crusade to help defend the city, and their wives and children…with the sun so high in the sky, the gates should be wide open to welcome the business we bring." He stopped and dropped his bundle of belongings. "Put your armour on."

The other Crusaders glared as they marched around them, but Melisende didn't dare disobey. If Zoticus was worried enough to put his own armour on, then she'd be a fool not to follow his example. She stuck her helm on her head, then struggled to pull her breastplate over it. Swearing, she took her helm off and tried again.

Screams came from the men ahead.

"Archers!" Zoticus hissed.

Melisende dropped her breastplate to look.

Riders poured onto the plain between the Crusaders and the city, sending a storm of arrows into their lines. They fell short of the spot where Zoticus and she stood, but it would not be long before the riders rode into range.

"You remember how you owe me a favour, Squire?" Zoticus asked.

Oh God. Melisende nodded mutely. She knew she was not going to like doing what he asked.

"Drop everything, and RUN, GIRL, RUN!"

Clad in little more than her tunic and hose, without any armour to speak of, Melisende obeyed. She fixed her gaze on the distant forest, and willed her legs to move.

The thunder of hooves behind her had a familiar ring. She dared a glance over her shoulder, and her fears were realised.

Pegasus galloped at full speed toward her.

But the mare's rider was the Raven Knight, followed by his friends, instead of her brother.

Hunt. Sport. A murdered girl. Realisation dawned on her that she'd become their quarry, while they forgot the battle that raged around them in their frenzy for the hunt.

But none of the knights knew she'd raced Pegasus since the mare had first learned to run. This was a race the mare could not win.

Melisende bit her lip, tasting the magic that coursed through her veins, and flew.

Eighteen

Melisende ran until she could run no more, and she was forced to lean against a tree as she fought to catch her breath. One, two, thr…

A man's scream behind her had her scrambling up the tree, heedless of the scratches from bark or branches until she reached a height where the leaves thinned and she could see through the canopy.

But what she saw…

The plain she'd looked upon only a moment before was now a heaving sea of blood, as two armies fought for supremacy and their lives, amid screams, growls and roars that seemed to belong more to beasts than to men. Yet the crunch of metal through bone and skin told the truth even to her unwilling ears. They were both beasts and men, armed with deadly weapons and battle rage no beast possessed.

Melisende wept for them, and for her vain hope that she might help this army. She wrapped her arms around her head, trying to muffle the sounds of battle or at least the agonised screams, but they echoed in her ears still.

Finally, her face pressed against the bark of a tree that bore witness to a battle she dared not watch, Melisende prayed to go home. She prayed with a fervour she had not known since she was a little girl, repeating the words until they turned into nonsense in her head, and still the battle raged.

Nineteen

Melisende woke unwillingly, her body feeling bruised as though she'd been thoroughly beaten. Even her face felt tender. Yet as she lifted her face from the hard surface she'd been resting against, she realised she was still in a tree, with the rough bark of the trunk still beneath her hands. How she'd slept through the remains of the battle, she did not know, but daylight faded into darkness, though it had not silenced the screams.

She stretched up, peering above the canopy at the battlefield she'd fled. To one side was a well-lit camp, with scattered campfires between the dark shadows she guessed were soldiers' tents. The screams she heard now came from women, likely the camp followers who had marched with the army and been captured upon their defeat. Some had been whores, while others were cooks and laundresses, servants pressed into service who did not deserve such a fate. Or perhaps they were women from the city, stolen before they'd shut the gates? She was under no illusions that the army she had marched with would have done any different. It was not religion that guided the soldiers' behaviour, she had learned along the way. If their superiors did not guard their appetites, neither would the men. Women were but possessions to them all, things to be had, whether they were willing or not. Her hand strayed to her belt, ready to draw her sword, but the scabbard was gone. Yet another thing she'd dropped in her headlong retreat. What she'd give for the last loaf of bread in her bag, or that cheese she'd been saving…

But her bag and all her other belongings

remained upon the battlefield, lost in the darkness. She could not look for them until day dawned, and when it did, the army would find her easy prey.

Like some sort of African ape, this tree had become her new home. Laughter threatened to erupt, but she stifled it. Darkness and silence were the only armour she had now. Too much noise would draw attention from the army camp.

She blinked. Was that a light she'd seen upon the battlefield? No, surely not. And yet...

There was another, and another! She counted more than a dozen before she began to look more closely. Each light was a small lantern, held low by men who leaned over the bodies of the newly fallen, patting down their pockets, putting things into a bag, sometimes even stealing the men's shoes, before moving onto the next.

Melisende recoiled in horror. Whoever they were, these men were looting the bodies of their valuables, stealing from those who could no longer protest.

A gurgling cry went up, and Melisende

watched in horror as the wounded man who had protested was stabbed to death before her eyes. He'd been Seljuk, not Crusader — so these thieves were not part of either army, so mercenary they would kill anyone for a few coins. Or this man's jewelled dagger, as it turned out. The weapon caught the light for barely a moment, before it was stuffed into a sack.

Melisende started in surprise. She recognised the sack, for the gay stripes had provoked much laughter from Zoticus when he'd seen it. He'd said that only a woman would choose a pretty sack instead of a plain one, but it appeared he'd been wrong. Thieves were partial to pretty things, too.

She hoped Zoticus had survived the battle. He'd saved her life, assassin or not. She didn't think he truly deserved to die so. The only way there would have been survivors was if they had run as she had.

She'd called it cowardice before, but now she was not so sure. There was no honour in what had been done to those men down there. Now they were being dishonoured in death, robbed of what little they possessed by a strange band of bandits.

She could hardly talk. She was trapped in a tree, with no food and nothing but her eating knife, and no idea where her next meal might come from or whether she'd ever make it home. Melisende wanted to weep but she had no tears left. For the first time, she understood the desire for vengeance that had burned in many Crusaders' words along the way. She wished she had the power to make all men regret the violence they brought to the world, but she was one girl, and they were out there in their thousands. So she fixed her ire upon one man – the thief who carried her striped sack. Her gaze followed him, as he crept from body to body, adding theft after theft to the crime she already condemned him for.

When his corpse robbing was complete, he would have to sleep some time. And when he did, she would use her dagger as Zoticus might have, and take back what was hers.

Twenty

When Mithra arrived at the gates the next morning with his handcart, he was surprised to find them still shut. Nor did the guards know when they would be allowed to open – the Seljuk army outside the walls gave the orders now.

So, with little else to do, Mithra ascended to the top of the walls again. He wasn't the only one who wanted to see what changes a night had wrought. Yet nothing had changed, or so it seemed.

All the bodies still lay where they had fallen

in battle, beginning to bloat in the blazing sun. The Seljuk army had camped by the river, as if they had never left. Nothing remained of the Crusader army.

Well, that was not entirely true. When the two armies had engaged yesterday, part of the Crusader column had broken off and retreated back the way they'd come. The Seljuks had been too busy celebrating their victory to bother going after the rest.

But even as the thought entered his mind, Mithra could see a peculiar procession leaving the army camp and heading for the gates. It started with soldiers, but the stumbling, shambling figures who followed them were a pitiful sight.

At first, Mithra thought that these were the same women they'd stolen from the city the last time they were here, but what remained of their clothes told a different story. These women had come with the Crusaders, and were now considered the spoils of war. More slaves for market, after a night of serving at enemy soldiers' pleasure. Dead eyed women who stared in horror at the carnage on the battlefield, cringing away from their captors, with nowhere to run.

"You may now open the gates," the new herald shouted. "But listen well. If there are any traitors still alive in Dorylaeum, we will seek you out. If you think to shelter one of these foul Crusaders who fled from battle, your fate will be the same as theirs." He pointed at the line of beaten women. "Your wives and children will be sold as slaves. These infidels will not befoul our lands again!"

The herald repeated his words several times, for the benefit of those on the walls or within the city. With every word, Mithra's fury grew. He strode down the steps, his lips pressed tight together so that his own words would not slip out. When the gates ground open, he was the first man through them, looking neither at the battlefield or the army he wished had died there. Finally, he reached the forest, where once again, he took his anger out on the trees. The sun shone above, but for him, the world had gone dark. He could not imagine a world worse than the one he lived in today.

Twenty-One

Dawn seemed to be an unspoken signal between the body thieves. As soon as the sun rose, so did they, melting into the trees before the stirring army camp could see them.

Melisende kept her eyes on her striped sack. She slid down her tree and started to follow them through the forest.

The men were weary from the long night's labour, and rarely looked around to see if anyone was following them. They walked and walked before finally they stopped in a clearing full of horses. Palfreys, destriers, plus a few geldings that looked to have come from her father's stock, they were so superior to the rest — these animals had belonged to Crusader knights, Melisende realised, though these magnificent mounts belonged to this pack of thieves now.

Yet the men moved past the horses, to part of the clearing when no grass grew. What Melisende at first took for a round hill was nothing of the sort. When her eyes adjusted to the gloom, she realised she regarded a large rock, but the thieves stood around it with some reverence.

"You! The traitorous battlefield wench!"

Melisende whirled in shock to find a man behind her. She bit her lip and raced up the nearest tree, faster than a cat.

She climbed until she'd reached what she felt was a safe height. Only then did she dare peer out again.

Instead of following her, the man had sunk to his knees. Only now did she see from his bloodstained tunic that this was not one of the thieves, but the Horn Knight. Somehow, he had survived the battle, and now he looked vainly about, searching for her.

Then the circle of thieves closed around him, and it didn't matter.

"The girl, the girl…!" he cried.

One of the thieves stepped forward, drew his sword, and thrust it through the man's throat. The Horn Knight gurgled for a moment, before his life left him.

Melisende held her breath. If this many men started looking for the girl he'd seen, she wasn't sure she could move fast enough to escape them all. Silence and stillness were her only weapons now.

The leader cleaned his sword on the former knight's tunic, then pointed at two of his men. "You and you. Search the body for anything of value. Then take the body back to the battlefield. We don't dare leave anything here to mark the spot."

The two men nodded and began the grisly task.

A moment later, a fight broke out between the two.

The leader stepped between them, demanding to know what was the matter.

"His signet ring is missing," one man said.

"Because you stole it!" the second man said.

"Not I! I'm the one who saw where the ring was on his finger, but there's nothing but pale skin now!"

"You're seeing things, you are!"

The leader held up his hands for silence. "What does it matter? All we have, belongs to us all. We add to the treasure left by our predecessors, and leave more for those who come after us. We are the Forty Thieves!"

The two men grumbled their agreement, finished robbing the man, then carried him between them out of clearing.

The rest of the thieves, including the man still carrying Melisende's striped sack, headed back to the rock. They all fell silent as the leader gave a command that sounded like, "Open something."

None of the men moved. Melisende shrugged, dismissing the man's order as gibberish, until she saw the rock begin to move. A house sized boulder rolled aside smoothly, as though some hidden machinery was at work. It left behind a hole several yards across, and Melisende glimpsed steps spiralling downward.

The thieves were not the slightest bit surprised, moving single file down the steps until the leader went last. He uttered another incantation that Melisende could not make out, before the boulder rolled back into its original place.

Dividing Melisende from everything she owned and the thief carrying it once more.

Twenty-Two

"Ho, woodcutter!"

More than anything, Mithra wanted to ignore the soldier and keep pushing his fully loaded handcart back to town. But the corpses staring up at the sky reminded him that doing so would only earn him a place among them.

Schooling his face into blankness, Mithra turned to face the man who'd shouted. "Yes?"

"How much for this cartload of wood?"

Mithra took a deep breath, doing the calculation in his head, before naming a price no sane man in the city would pay.

He had it in his hands before he could blink.

"The same again for every load you can bring before dark. The General wants these bodies burned."

Mithra nodded and thanked the man, even as the words seemed to choke him, then beat a hasty retreat for the forest. He'd bring one more load, after dark, and steer as far away from the army camp as he could when he brought it.

And in between, he'd hide deep in the forest, where no soldier would bother following him.

He found himself following a trail that some beast had made, which was barely wide enough to allow the cart to pass. More than once, it caught in the undergrowth and he had to hack at grasping branches that hoped to steal the cart from him.

Finally, he emerged into a clearing filled with horses.

"What in heaven's name…"

The words came from a woman, he was certain of it, though Mithra could not see her.

Then a body crashed into his, knocking him

to the ground. He scrambled to his feet in time to see his cart shoved behind some bushes before the girl returned.

"I thought you were them returning. Quick, hide, they can't be far!" she urged, setting off at a run for a tree on the other side of the clearing.

Mithra couldn't seem to move, for he was too busy staring. She looked like one of the captured Crusader women who'd been paraded past the walls that very morning, yet she had somehow missed out on their fate. Likely she'd run away into the woods, and they'd lost her in the dark.

He understood why she'd want to hide, but the soldiers knew he was here to collect wood. If they'd followed him, then he needed to get his cart out of that bush and set to work with his axe.

"Do you want to die?" the girl demanded. Out of nowhere, she crashed into him again, somehow pushing him up against a tree. Her slight body pressed against his could not possess the necessary strength for such a thing, and yet Mithra could not deny she had done it.

Up close, he could not help but stare at her face. Even as she glared at him, he had to admit she was pretty.

He opened his mouth to tell her so.

She muttered an oath he'd never heard a woman utter before, and clamped her hand over his mouth, shaking her head.

Only then did Mithra hear the sound of approaching footsteps. Two men, dressed like ordinary Dorylaeum citizens. Except ordinary citizens did not carry curved swords.

Wide-eyed, he pulled the girl closer, twisting his body so that it shielded hers.

She'd had the courage to escape the army once. That made her a thousand times braver than he'd ever be. Crusader maiden or not, he would not let them capture her again. He might not be able to save Peter's family or any of the other women, but this time would be different.

Twenty-Three

Heaven help her, but Melisende had never been this close to a man before. Well, except maybe her brothers in the practice ring, until they'd learned that greater strength in close combat was no match for her well-placed foot and the power she could put behind it.

But this wasn't the same.

He was dressed like one of the thieves, which is why she'd taken him for one of them at first, but the barrow he'd been pushing looked like something the farmers back home used to take their cabbages to market.

And just like the peasants back home, he didn't carry any weapons.

Curse her soft heart, but she did not want to see him die as the Horn Knight had. So she'd used her magic to move him. Now he knew more about her than her own father and brothers. And his body was pressed against hers, nothing but two thin tunics between them that the heat of their bodies made feel like nothing at all.

He had a firm, muscled body, this peasant, if that was what he was. He worked hard at whatever he did. He could have used his strength against her, but he did not take advantage of their closeness. Even the look in his eyes lacked the lust she might have expected. His eyes darted back to the clearing when he heard the two thieves approach, and he became as still as the tree they had chosen for their hiding place.

"What's the password again?" one man asked.

"Open…simsi!" he said, or at least that's what Melisende thought she heard.

The man beside her stiffened as he saw the

boulder move. He did not relax until they uttered the evidently magical password again and the boulder closed the entrance to their cave.

"Did you see that?" he breathed.

She gave a sharp nod. "That's the second time I've seen it. The first time was earlier today, when the rest of their band of thieves arrived and went in. I think their chief said there were forty of them, though I didn't think to count them. Then one of the knights who'd fled into the woods when the battle started happened upon them, and they killed him. Those two took his body back to the others. If they found you, they would have killed you just as easily, I am certain."

The man stepped back and bowed. "Then I owe you my life, though I don't even know your name."

She hesitated. Godfrey was gone and so was Zoticus. Did she need to invent a false name, or was she far enough from home that her own would sound false?

Finally, she said, "I am Lady Melisende of Mareschal. I rode with the Crusaders until someone killed them."

A faint blush coloured his cheeks. "So I must offer you my condolences for Lord Mareschal…?"

She laughed. "There is no such lord. My father is Baron of Mareschal. Of all the men who died here yesterday, I only knew one of them well, and I'm not certain even an army could kill him. If he did survive, I'm sure he's far from here already."

The man nodded. "I am Mithra of Dorylaeum, son of Ali Baba from the same city. I am delighted to meet you, Lady Melisende. Did you know you share your name with the Crusader queen, who lives and rules in what you call the Holy City?"

Queen Melisende. No, she had not. "I'm not her," Melisende said.

"No, you are younger and more beautiful," Mithra said.

Now it was her turn to blush. Then a thought struck her. "Do you know her? Perhaps if I could see her, speak to her, she might help me find a way home."

Mithra hung his head. "I fear I have never

met a queen, nor been allowed to speak to one. Even if I did know her, I could not take you to her, for there is an army between here and my home. If any soldier saw you…"

"He'd throw me over his shoulder and dump me in the place they're keeping their other prisoners. Their whores," Melisende spat.

"Their slaves," Mithra corrected. "They take the women and children they capture to sell as slaves."

Somehow, Melisende wasn't sure whether that was better or worse.

A rumble shook the ground beneath them. The boulder was moving again.

"Quick, they're coming out. Hide," she said, climbing the nearest tree.

Mithra sprang up beside her, climbing like he was half monkey. Maybe he was.

"I had no idea Crusader ladies could climb trees as well as a woodcutter," Mithra whispered.

"I grew up with a bunch of older brothers, whose every game was to see who could be the fastest, the strongest, the best." She shrugged.

"I was the smallest, and the only girl. While never the strongest, I could always climb the highest. It helped no end when I began to learn how to heal, and prepare medicines. Sometimes the best leaves were only to be found at the top of a tree, and there are certain parasitic herbs that twine up a tree so that the only place to collect them is high above the ground. What my brothers didn't realise is that every hour spent in the stillroom or the sickroom is only after many hours spent in the forests and fields – "

She fell silent as the thieves began to emerge.

When they headed for the horses, she searched for the one with her striped sack, but every man was empty handed. Which meant her things were still inside the cave.

Once again, the leader was last, muttering his magic words to close the cave behind him.

"Where to next, Captain?" one thief asked.

The leader thought for a moment, then said, "With armies marching along the trade routes, no merchant will venture out, so all our usual haunts will have slim pickings until the war is done. So, we follow the remnants of the Crusader army. Some of them were surely wounded, and they'll fall behind. We can pick them off as they do. When they next go into battle, we'll be there to take first pick of both what's on the bodies and in the baggage train."

Disgusting scavengers. Preying upon wounded men and fallen soldiers. If bandits like these ever entered her father's lands, her brothers would scour them from the earth. She wished she could do the same here.

If only she were a powerful enchantress, capable of casting spells that incapacitated dozens of men at a time. Or that could turn the tide of battle, transforming defeat into victory.

Instead, even when she did use her magic, she'd managed to lose her last loaf of bread to a common thief.

The thieves mounted up and rode out, walking their horses in single file along a game trail until Melisende could no longer hear the unhurried hoofbeats.

"I counted forty of them. Did you?" Mithra asked.

She'd been so busy raging against them, she'd forgotten to count the thieves. Put to shame by a common woodcutter.

Melisende confessed that she'd been too distracted to do so.

Mithra gave her a sympathetic nod, his eyes dark with concern. "You've been through quite an ordeal. When I think of the other women…why, you are quite remarkable."

Other women now in the hands of the enemy. Women the Crusader knights should have protected, instead of running away like the honourless cowards they were. This crusade was doomed to fail from the beginning. She should not have come.

"Don't cry," Mithra said. "Here, don't you want to see what those thieves keep in their secret cave?"

Actually, she did not much care. Except that her own things were there…

Melisende wiped her eyes. Crying was for children. "We should wait to make sure they don't return. It would not do to be found inside, for surely that boulder is the only way in or out."

Mithra's eyes grew wide. "I had not thought of that. Best we wait, then, as you say, wise Lady Melisende."

That made her laugh. She definitely wasn't wise. Then again, the man might be teasing her. He looked to be about the same age as her brothers, and they liked to tease her all the time.

"If I was so wise, I would have stayed home, instead of coming here on this foolish crusade," she said.

Mithra looked thoughtful. "My master used to say wisdom comes from experience, making mistakes that you must learn from. The wisest men have made many mistakes."

"Master? Are you a slave?"

Mithra stared at her for a long moment, before he said, "Things must be very different in the north, if you cannot tell the difference between a slave and a free man. Though I suppose being an apprentice is a little like being a slave, for my father paid my master to teach me his trade, which meant working very hard without being paid."

"But...you are a man now, too old to be an

apprentice, surely. Most of the boys back home became journeymen younger than my brother was when he was made a squire."

Mithra nodded. "In some trades, it is so. The trade guilds say who is good enough to become a master, but not all trades have a guild in Dorylaeum. Without a guild, we are all either apprentices or merchants. Perhaps if my master had lived a little longer, he would have helped me to become a merchant. Or his son, who would happily have partnered with me in a trade venture."

"How did they die?" Melisende asked.

Mithra's expression darkened. "It is a dark tale, one not fit for a woman's ears, but when the woman has been in battle and survived to tell the tale…perhaps you are made of sterner stuff than the norm."

Melisende didn't think he'd be as impressed if he knew she'd run, climbed a tree and slept through most of the battle, so she merely said, "Tell me."

By the time Mithra told her about his master's death, she wished she could hide her face and weep for these men she had not known. But there was worse to come.

The Seljuks sounded no better than the men she'd marched with.

"Peter counted on the Crusaders to come and save him. Perhaps it is for the best that he did not live to see their defeat," Mithra said sadly.

"I'm not sure any more that a crusade can save anyone. Saving a city by sacking it and killing the inhabitants…I fear they are all mad!"

"So you have no desire to rejoin the crusade, if you could?" Mithra asked.

Melisende shook her head. "The only thing I want now is to go home."

Twenty-Four

The silence stretched between them, but Mithra did not know how to break it. If he was trapped in a foreign land, far from home, hiding from an army that wanted to torture and enslave him, he didn't think he would have her calm composure. He'd be anxious to take action, leaving caution behind in the dust, and probably get himself killed.

Yet Melisende had kept them both alive.

"It's been some time. When they left, they talked of catching up to the rest of the Crusader army. They would have had to hurry.

It should be safe to see what they keep in their cave now," Melisende said, descending.

He'd been so busy talking to her, he'd completely forgotten about his own curiosity. He mumbled his agreement and climbed down after her.

Lady Melisende moved to stand in the same spot where the thief captain had, took a deep breath, and said, "Open simsi."

Nothing happened.

Melisende cleared her throat with some annoyance. Louder this time, she repeated, "Open simsi."

The boulder did not move.

Most girls he knew would have given way to anger by now, or at least stamped their feet, but Lady Melisende merely took another breath and asked, "Is there something else the man did to make it open?"

Mithra shrugged. "I think he only said something." She'd been here longer, and heard the incantation more times than he had, so surely she knew it better.

"Perhaps…perhaps it's blood magic, which requires a blood price to work," she said. She took her dagger, pressed the point to her finger and waited until a drop of blood welled up. Then she wiped it on the rock. "Open simsi."

Still nothing.

Finally, Mithra said, "I thought he said sesame. You know, like the seed."

She looked puzzled. "What sort of seed?"

"Sesame seed. You know, it's small and straw-coloured. You can press them to make oil that's good to cook with, or you can use the seeds in cooking. Mixed with honey and spices, some of the bakers in town make the most delicious cakes…" He opened his eyes to find her staring at her. "You don't know sesame?"

Melisende shook her head. "We don't have that sort of seed at home. Besides, why would he talk about seeds when he wants a massive rock to move? Simsi is the old word for mountain where I come from. So when he said, 'Open simsi,' he's telling the mountain to open. Isn't there some sort of proverb about mountains moving for a particular prophet? It makes much more sense."

Mithra had to admit what she said was true,

but the unmoving stone seemed to say otherwise. "I still think I heard sesame," he said.

"Then you try to command the boulder," Melisende said, folding her arms across her breast.

Mithra did not want to look like a fool, but he wasn't sure he had a choice. The rock hadn't moved for her, so the worst that could happen would be that he might fail, too.

What did it matter? She probably didn't think much of him, anyway. He was nothing but a lowly woodcutter, while she was a lady who lived in some Crusader castle, far to the north, protected by her knightly brothers.

Who would likely run him through with their swords if they saw him speaking to their sister.

Mithra sighed. "Open sesame," he said.

The rock gave an ominous rumble, then rolled aside.

Mithra looked around, worried that someone might have heard it, and know that intruders were about to enter their cave. But no one came.

"I'll go first, shall I? After all, that's best, just in case they've left a guard inside," Mithra said, brandishing his axe as if he was eager to meet his foe, when that was definitely not the case.

But no matter what fear he felt, he could not allow her to come to more danger because of him. He'd opened the cave, after all.

Not waiting for Melisende's assent, he descended into the dark.

Twenty-Five

As she headed down the steps, at first Melisende wished she'd brought a lantern, for if this place was anything like the cellars back home, she would be standing in the pitch dark within a few yards of the bottom of the stairs. But this cave was no cellar, for it seemed that the thieves had left the lantern burning when they'd left.

Did that mean they had left a guard with it?

Fear almost drove her back up the steps to the surface, but she dared not show cowardice in front of the woodcutter. Especially as he walked in front of her, so he would bear the brunt of any attack.

If anything, the cave brightened, the further she walked into it. Yet the lights seemed to come from a dozen different places, all up near the ceiling. When she held her hand up near one, she was surprised to feel a draught creeping down her fingers. She marvelled at the thought that air and light could come from the surface that were invisible to those who walked above. If anyone had known such a wondrous cavern lay beneath, they surely would have tried to find a way inside.

"Can you believe it?" Mithra stood with his arms outspread, his eyes wide with wonder.

Melisende smiled, biting back a comment that the cellars in Dorylaeum were evidently much smaller than those back home.

Instead, she scanned the underground chamber, searching for her things. Finally, she glimpsed the coloured stripes, hiding beneath several other sacks that looked dull in comparison.

She struggled to shove them aside, before getting her hands on the striped sack and pulling it from beneath its drab fellows.

It was heavier than she remembered, likely full of things looted from the battlefield bodies. Having no desire for stolen treasures, Melisende upended her bag on the stone floor. Coins cascaded out – copper, silver, and more gold than she remembered possessing at the beginning of her journey. Jewelled daggers and brooches made up the rest, with no sign of her spare clothes, or her sword.

Her stomach growled a reminder of what else was missing.

Oh, that vile thief! She pawed through the tinkling hoard, but still she didn't find what she sought. Instead, she swore.

"What is the matter?" Mithra asked.

"That ill begotten whoreson stole my cheese!"

Mithra burst out laughing. "Truly, I have never heard a woman use language so colourful. And what do you care for some old cheese? There is enough gold here to buy you a lifetime's worth of cheese, and all the cheese your children could ever want, too."

Melisende blinked. She rose from her

crouch and surveyed the room properly for the first time. As she took in what she had missed while intent on the search for her sack, her eyes grew wide. "It must have taken more than one band of thieves to amass this much wealth," she said. "Not even a dozen such bands in their entire lifetime…"

The plain sacks she'd shifted had started to spill out their contents. Each held a fortune in gold and jewels. Yet they were stacked higher than her head, and wider than her arms could reach. Gold statues gleamed in the far corner, looking at first like men, until she looked more closely and realised they bore the heads of beasts. Chests and jars and barrels, stacked a dozen deep, reached almost to the ceiling of the cavern. On all sides, she saw the wealth of more than a dozen kings' treasuries, with dozens more hiding in the shadows.

Melisende pressed her lips together. "I don't care where they got it. I don't care how many years they've been collecting it. They stole my things, and as I can't take them back, I shall fill the bag they stole from me with their gold, to pay for what they took." She began picking up the coins from the pile on the floor, flicking aside the jewels. She was no grave robber. When she was done with the gold, she started on the silver.

"In payment for the cheese," she said.

Then the coppers.

"For my loaf of bread, and my cloak."

When there were no more coins on the floor, she tied the sack shut and rose, throwing it over her shoulder. "The gold should pay for my passage home, with a little left over for a bath and a meal and a night in a real bed in your city's best inn. If you can recommend one, I would be grateful," she said.

Once again, she found Mithra staring at her. "All this wealth does not belong to anyone. You said it yourself – these thieves stole it. With just a small part of this, you could live comfortably without having to work another day of your life." He shook his head. "And yet you take one bag, and copper coins for bread?"

It was Melisende's turn to stare. No amount of money could stop her from having to work every day of her life. Not for money or reward, but because it was expected of her. A woman in her position had the responsibility of looking after the people on her father's – or her husband's – estate. Hours spent in the stillroom, drying herbs or preparing medicines. Hours more seeing to the sick, and bringing charity to those who needed it. Her father's horse herds and the tithes from their tenants bought them everything they needed, but no amount of money could buy good health. That took time and care and more than a little love. Yet this man from a faraway land knew nothing of her life at home. She did not know where to start to even try to make him understand. "What would you do with it, then?" she challenged.

His eyes gleamed in the darkness. "I would buy a house for my father and mother, so they need not ever pay rent again to a greedy landlord. I would pay the food merchants in the marketplace to deliver provisions to their house every week, so that they would never have to go hungry again. I would tell the inn where my mother works to hire a new cook, so that the only people my mother would cook for, and then only if she wishes it, would be my father and me. If she did not want to cook any more, I would hire a woman to do it for her. Or a girl she might train as her apprentice, perhaps. I would pay for two orphaned boys to be my father's apprentices, to help him cut and fetch firewood until they were old enough to do the job on their own, so that my father need no longer work. I would go to all the merchants my master traded with, and start doing business with them once again. I would take apprentices of my own, bright, poor boys, or those with no parents, and no hope of someone paying for them to have an apprenticeship, so that they might learn the trade as I did. If it were possible, I would pay every soldier in that army up there to desert their General and go home, never to take up arms again. And I would travel to Rialto, to see my master's family, to tell them what happened to Simon and Peter and the others, and give them what gold I managed to salvage before the army stole all their worldly goods." Mithra took a deep breath, then let it out slowly, as if he had so many things in his mind, he had to pause to decide what to say next.

"Then you should take it," she said. "But if those soldiers are anything like the crusading army I marched with, no amount of coin given them will ever be enough. They wish to take, and conquer, and they will not stop, not even if God himself commanded it. So do all the good you can, but I pray, do not give a single copper coin to those soldiers. Or the Crusaders, if they ever return. Hide it until they are gone, and use the money to repair the damage they have done." She closed her eyes. "All I ask is that you help me buy passage home."

Mithra nodded gravely. "You have saved my life. I can refuse you nothing. I will do everything in my power to help you find hospitality in my city, and, after that, a way home."

His words were spoken like an oath, and she believed them.

"I will go now, and return in the morning," he said. "Here, take this." He held out a small pouch that had been fastened to his belt. "It was to be my midday meal. I'm sure it is poor fare for a lady such as yourself, and I will see that you have better when you enter the city, but I hope it may tide you over until I can find a way to sneak you past the army camp without being captured."

He took a bag of coins on his way out, hiding it under a load of fresh cut wood Melisende helped him stack on his handcart before he left.

Wrapped in a cloak she'd borrowed from the cavern, Melisende curled up in a tree with broad enough branches to cradle her body safely, and settled in for what she hoped would be her last night sleeping outside.

Twenty-Six

Grabbing a handful of coins from the bag before stashing it beneath a pile of firewood, Mithra headed first for the market. If Lady Melisende meant to enter the city, she would need to look like a local woman. There was a merchant who sold secondhand clothes which might be suitable.

He picked the first three gowns he saw, all the sort of thing his mother might wear, and added a couple of veils. He debated whether to buy some sort of underdress, too, but just the thought of Lady Melisende wearing nothing more than one of those thin, filmy things made him blush, so he decided against it. Let her buy her own underthings, for she had no shortage of coin. The thing was to get her into the city.

Ah, but she'd wanted a cloak, too, he remembered. He found one that was the same shade of green as her eyes, and added that to his pile.

The merchant who owned the shop never took his eyes off Mithra for a moment. As though he expected him to try to steal his shabby stock. Mithra wanted to tell the man that he could afford to take Lady Melisende to the silk merchant at the other end of the bazaar, but he restrained himself. He'd pay for his purchases, then go and see if the inn up in the Merchants' Quarter had any rooms free.

"How much?" Mithra asked, reaching into his money pouch.

The merchant lifted each item, eyed it for a long moment, before setting it down and going to the next, as though he hadn't watch Mithra select every one. Finally, he rested one hand on the pile of clothes and stretched out the other, palm up. "Fifty coppers," he said loftily.

Mithra thought it sounded a little high, but then he'd never bought women's clothing before. He didn't have time to haggle. He took out a coin and set it on the table.

The merchant's eyes grew wide. He snatched up the coin, then bit it.

Too late, Mithra realised he'd pulled out gold instead of silver. He dug through his pouch and pulled out a handful of copper. "Here…"

"Thief! A lowly labourer like you could not come upon gold like this honestly. I knew you were a thief the moment I saw you. Guard, guard!"

Instead of a guard, the merchant had managed to get the attention of a pair of soldiers, who hurried over.

Mithra swore, threw the coins back into his pouch, and bolted.

At first, he ran through the middle of the market, dodging between people until he found the alley he wanted. He dived for the narrow gap between one shop and another, then headed into the maze of alleys and back passages that only a boy who'd grown up in the bazaar truly knew. The soldiers lost him in seconds, and by the time he emerged from the side door of Simon's old shop, wearing the set of clean clothes he'd kept there when he worked in the shop, they were nowhere in sight.

Holding his head proudly like the merchant he'd once hoped to become, he headed for the inn.

The taproom was almost empty, but for two soldiers who eyed him suspiciously when he entered. "Are you new to the city?" one of them asked.

They both had their hands on their swords, as if waiting for him to deliver a less than favourable answer.

"No, I was born here," Mithra said easily. "I worked in one of the shops a few doors down, until we had to close because we'd run out of goods to sell. I'm expecting a new shipment of silk and spices from the east soon, and I wanted to see if there would be any rooms free for the caravan master when he arrives."

"All the rooms are free," said the innkeeper, with a surly glance at the soldiers. "We've had no new guests since the army arrived, and all the old ones left. Your friend will be assured of the best room in the house. As long as he doesn't mind answering a lot of questions from these men first."

Mithra's heart sank. If Lady Melisende came here, the soldiers would capture her for sure. He managed a smile. "I shall tell him when he arrives."

It was the same at the next inn, and the next, right down to the cheap one by the gates where his mother worked.

Darkness was falling, and he had no clothes for Melisende, and nowhere for her to sleep.

Perhaps his aunt might have some old clothes that Melisende might be able to wear. Praying his luck would change, Mithra headed for his uncle's house.

To his surprise, Aunt Seda answered the door.

"What happened to the maid?" Mithra asked.

Seda frowned. "The girl ran away. I don't know what's the trouble with these modern girls, not wanting to do good, honest work.

One night she was here, and the next morning – gone! Now I need a new one and I don't know where to find one. I don't suppose you know of any girls where you live who are good workers?"

Most of the girls where Mithra lived were all good workers, spending every hour of the day working at whatever jobs they already had, if they weren't taking care of their family. Sometimes, like his mother, they did both. None of them were in need of another job.

"If I do, I shall send her straight to you, dear aunt," Mithra promised.

She smiled. "You always were a good boy. If only Kasim and I could have had a son like you…"

"My mother sent me to ask if you have any old clothes you no longer need. There are a couple of poor widows near us who are dependent on the kindness of the city, as they have no family to care for them…"

Seda nodded. "Of course, of course. Perhaps you can help me lift the lids on the chests, for I have no maid to do it for me now."

Mithra dutifully followed his aunt inside and helped her search through her clothes until he had an armful of things that might fit Melisende.

"Oh, and there are these things of Kasim's which no longer fit him. I fear he's grown quite stout, and I've had to order new tunics from the tailor's for him. A new belt, too, for he cannot fasten the old one. It's still quite fine. I'm sure it would fit you."

His aunt would not let him go until he'd at least fastened the new belt around his waist, and then she fussed about him, shifting things from his old belt to the new one. He reached for his coin pouch at the same time as she did, spilling the contents everywhere.

Seda whispered a gentle oath – not the sort that burned his ears, like Melisende's – and knelt to help him collect the coins.

When he had everything back where it belonged, Mithra thanked his aunt, bundled up the clothes into an old sack, and headed home.

Now night had fallen, he saw more soldiers in the streets, but he just bowed his head, like any tired labourer at the end of a long day, and they mostly ignored him.

Lady Melisende had no hope of hiding in Dorylaeum with all these soldiers around. They would know her for a Crusader maiden in a moment.

But if they thought she was a lowly servant, someone beneath their notice, she might have a chance.

An idea began to form in the back of his mind. By morning, he hoped to have the whole scheme thought out, before he presented it to Melisende and prayed she would agree to it.

Twenty-Seven

"I don't believe a simple change of clothes will convince them I'm not a Crusader," Melisende said, looking down at the shapeless dress with distaste.

"Says the Crusader maiden who made an entire army think she was a boy for the march here," Mithra returned.

That made her pause. "Are people really so silly that they only see what is on the surface?" It was a sobering thought, and a saddening one.

"People see what they expect to see.

Soldiers expected to see a boy in armour, marching with them, and so that's what they saw. The Dorylaeum guards expect to see a modestly clad woman, escorted by her husband or brother or whoever, as do the Seljuk soldiers. If you wear this, they will take one look and dismiss you as beneath their notice."

"Men always notice women. Sometimes they try to hide it, but, trust me, we know when we are being watched."

Mithra blushed. "I only glanced over my shoulder to see if you were finished dressing. When I realised you were not, I turned my back again."

Melisende's mouth dropped open in surprise. More at his honesty than his admission. She gave herself a mental shake, telling herself he couldn't have seen much more than her bare back, for she'd turned her back on him, too, and…oh, what did it matter, anyway? She'd be headed home soon and she'd never see this woodcutter again.

"Let's go," he said, giving his handcart a push.

Panic rose up in her throat, but she forced it down. If Mithra had wanted to betray her to the soldiers, he'd have done so yesterday, without coming back and bringing her these scratchy clothes. With her hair covered by one veil and another that hid most of her face, there was nothing for the soldiers to see except a walking sack. She felt like a leper.

She glanced nervously at the army camp as they stepped out of the shadow of the forest. If they caught her, they certainly wouldn't treat her like a leper. Lecherous soldiers couldn't keep their hands off the women they had caught. Not to mention wearing what felt like a tent that ballooned around her while she walked would make it harder to run if she had to. Even with her magic, could she reach the cover of the trees?

"Keep your eyes on the ground. Pretend you're so painfully shy that you can't bear to see someone looking at you. Hunch your shoulders a little, and bow your head, like you're afraid of being beaten. Don't look around, don't stare, and definitely don't meet anyone's gaze.."

She aimed a glare at the back of his head before doing as he commanded. If her brothers could see her now, they would laugh so hard they pissed themselves. She bowed her head to no one, and to do it now on the orders of some foreign peasant…if her life did not depend on it, she wasn't sure she could bear it.

It took an eternity to cross the battlefield, even with the bodies gone. She didn't dare wonder where they'd gone.

Finally, they slowed as they reached the gates.

"Good evening," Mithra said.

The guards returned his greeting, and they exchanged pleasantries for a moment until someone said, "Who's the girl?"

A tug on her sleeve made her shuffle closer to the handcart. She relaxed a little when she realised it was Mithra, then tensed again under the guards' sudden scrutiny.

"This is my betrothed, Melis. She came to find me to invite me to dinner with her family, and she was afraid to walk back through the forest on her own, so she waited to walk with me."

One of the guards sniggered, while the other laughed aloud. "Oh, it's called walking, now, is it?"

Mithra lifted his shoulders in a shrug. "Well, our families won't let us wed yet, what with the war and all, and we've been waiting so long...what else is a man to do but go for a walk in the woods?"

More laughter as the guards waved them through, wishing him a hasty wedding.

Melisende's face burned. If she meet anyone's eyes now, they'd see her mortification. Much safer to keep her gaze firmly on the ground.

When they were far enough away from the gate for no one to hear, she hissed, "Damn your impertinent hide, Mithra. Now everyone thinks I am your whore! I should strike you down for that. Were my brothers here, they would cut out your lying tongue."

Mithra kept his voice low. "No, they do not. Those two guards believe you are my betrothed, soon to be my obedient bride. From the moment I told them you were mine, they averted their eyes and looked only at me."

"They think we fornicated in the forest!" she persisted.

"Would you rather they knew the truth?"

No, for it would mean her death, and likely his as well.

"Take me to the inn. I want to wash," she snapped.

He hesitated for a moment, then said, "Come with me while I take my cart home, and then I shall take you to where you can stay."

She followed him to the door of what she might have called a tiny cottage, were the roof made of thatch and not stone. He tucked the handcart into a corner of the yard, then led the way down a new street.

The hovels on either side did not give the air of a prosperous place to stay.

"Are you sure the best inn is this way?" she demanded.

Mithra sighed. "Indeed it is, but I cannot take you there, nor to any other inn in the city, for there are soldiers waiting at all of them to put any newcomer to the question. A woman travelling alone is unusual enough, but one who arrives now, when there are no travellers left in the city…you would be caught and questioned for certain. So, in the absence of a suitable inn, I have found somewhere you might stay without suspicion until the army departs and you can seek passage home."

They passed several soldiers along the way, some of whom appeared to be patrolling, while others seemed to be looking for some off-duty entertainment.

She had to wait until the soldiers were far enough away before she said tartly, "It had better not be a brothel."

"Though you swear like one of their best customers, no, I would not dream of taking you to such a place."

Somewhat satisfied, she followed him through the poor district and into one that looked more prosperous.

"This is more like it," she said, looking at the larger houses with satisfaction.

Mithra chose one and rapped smartly at the door.

A well-dressed woman wearing a veil much like Melisende's answered it. "Good evening, nephew."

"Aunt Seda, this is Melis, the maid you wanted. She is formerly from a Crusader household, so she might not be as familiar with our ways, but she is capable and a quick learner. If you can give her somewhere suitable to sleep, she will serve you well."

Melisende did not have more than a moment to collect her wits before the woman had grabbed her arm and dragged her inside, closing the door on Mithra's only mildly apologetic countenance.

A maid? Truly? And shortening her name, so it sounded like malice. Perhaps she should have let the thieves kill him after all.

Twenty-Eight

When Mithra reached home, he found both his parents waiting for him, with a familiar sack on the table between them.

"Mother!" he said with surprise. "Does no one at the Gatehouse want supper tonight? I can't remember the last time you came home so early."

"No one at the Gatehouse wants a cook tonight, or any other night," Mother said. "With few visitors to the city and people scared to go out after dark on account of all the soldiers in the streets, the innkeeper's wife will do all their cooking from now on. I thought perhaps I could help you and your father, at least until there are travellers on the roads again, but when I went into the storeroom to fetch the handcart, I found this." She pointed at the sack.

His father took up the tale. "When I arrived home, your mother asked me about it, but I'd never seen it before. I certainly hadn't put it there, or carefully hidden it beneath a pile of fresh cut firewood. And when we opened it…" He tipped it up and gold cascaded across the table. "I know you sold Simon's goods and keep the money you made from them in a chest, but the dust atop it tells me you haven't touched that in weeks, and even if you sold every item in his warehouses, you could not have amassed so much gold. If it were filled with coppers, maybe, or even a few silver coins, but gold…this is a king's ransom here. Tell me – did you steal the Seljuk army's war chest?"

He wished he had, for without money, surely the soldiers would have to go home. But Mithra did not dare lie to his parents.

"I was cutting wood in the forest yesterday," he began.

He told them everything about the thieves, their magic cave, and all it contained. The only detail he left out was any mention of Lady Melisende.

Though she likely wouldn't forgive him for making her work as his aunt's maid, she definitely would not forgive him if she shared her secrets.

When Mithra had finished his tale, his father said, "My son, you have done a terrible thing. While there is little crime in stealing from a thief, the Forty Thieves are known for their ruthless methods and the power of their vengeance. If they find out you have taken what belongs to them, they will hunt you to the very ends of the earth, kill you, and slaughter everyone you have ever known or loved. To protect us from their wrath, we must bury the gold deep in the garden, and no one must ever know we have it."

In vain did Mithra argue that the coin could be spent in such a way without revealing the source of their wealth, but his parents would hear none of it.

On the morrow, both he and his father went out to cut wood again, for all the world as if nothing had changed.

And for a time, it seemed that little had. But not for long.

Twenty-Nine

To her surprise, Melisende found that being Seda's maid was not so onerous a job as it seemed. The thin pallet she was expected to sleep on was as uncomfortable as any of the nights she'd spent sleeping on the ground near Zoticus, but her duties seemed to consist solely of fetching and carrying things for either the cook or Seda herself.

Back at home, as mistress of the stillroom and succourer of the sick, she'd been far busier.

While she stayed inside the house, she

wasn't expected to wear the heavy veil she'd donned to get through the gates, and the cook seemed resigned to having to explain even the simplest task to her. Apparently, the woman had trained a great many maids.

Every day, she was expected to sweep the steps, and she took a moment to ascertain whether there were soldiers still patrolling the streets, or whether she might leave. Every day, she found them still there, so when she was finished, she headed back inside again, to fetch some meat for the cook, or to find the slippers Seda had lost since putting them down only a moment ago.

One day melted into the next, and she was surprised to discover she'd been a servant for more than two weeks before she met the master of the house, who'd been travelling to another town to see what had become of a shipment of trade goods which had not yet arrived.

He was a great, lumpy jelly of a man, with greedy eyes that matched his girth. His gaze touched on everything and made her feel like scrubbing.

He had a manservant who served his dinner, but the cook still expected her to carry the platters to the table, and Melisende felt his eyes on her every time she entered the room.

She was glad when the cook let her retire as soon as she'd brought in dessert, for with Master Kasim home, the evening meal would end quite late and it was better to wash the dishes in the morning, when they'd had time to soak.

Only that morning, she'd discovered a plentiful supply of straw in the hayloft above the stables, and after several trips from the loft to her tiny bedchamber, she now had a bed even her brothers would envy.

She fell asleep almost instantly, only to wake in the dark with her heart pounding and no reason for it that she could see.

Then she heard heavy breathing when she knew she was holding her breath.

She was up and out of bed in an instant, trying to escape from her tiny room, but a solid shadow blocked the doorway.

A shadow that shoved her up against the wall.

"Take those clothes off, girl," a male voice said.

A draught chilled her legs as she realised he'd seized hold of the hem of her gown and was trying to haul it up over her head.

"Go to hell," she snarled, tearing out of his grasp.

Then his full weight hit her, knocking her to the floor. He forced his lips against hers, in a slobbery kiss that made her retch.

She bit him.

He howled and lashed out at her, but she smashed her knee into his groin and fought her way free before any of his blows landed.

Then she bit her own lip, and magic seemed to infuse the air around her. She moved while it did not.

"Come back here, girl. I am the master of this house, and you will obey me!" Kasim roared.

"Touch me again and I'll cut off your wizened little prick, and shove it so far up your arse, all you'll taste for the next month will be your own balls," Melisende hissed, drawing her dagger.

He staggered to his feet, blundering past her in the dark toward his own chamber.

She breathed a sigh of relief and sheathed her dagger.

"I'll be back with my belt, and when I do, you'll learn obedience, bitch!" Kasim shouted.

Not bloody likely.

She paused only to pull on her boots and grab her cloak to cover herself before she raced out into the street. She wasn't sure where she was headed, but anywhere was better than here.

Thirty

Melisende stopped to catch her breath, and discovered she'd run clean across town to Mithra's house. She found him asleep in a loft above the storerooms, so she shook him awake.

Before he had time to speak, she said, "Did you know that your uncle is a lecherous toad who deserves to burn in hell for all eternity for trying to use his servants like whores?"

Mithra managed to sit up. "I had heard that he beat some of his servants, but I never imagined the beatings were anything but deserved. From what my aunt said…"

"Seda is a simpering fool who spends her days making clothes for the children she'll never have because her husband is too busy forcing himself on his servants in their own beds to spend any time in hers!"

"Well, we did suspect there was no love between them and he only married her for her father's money, but Seda is the only person I knew who would take you in without asking questions, even if it meant you had to pretend to be her maid for a few days. I'd hoped the army might leave before now, but they seem determined to stay. I'm as trapped as you, Melisende – I don't know what else to do."

She forced her hands down by her sides, in an effort to resist shaking Mithra again. Perhaps he truly didn't know what a villain his uncle was, or he hadn't until now. Seda's house had been a suitable place to hide, if Kasim hadn't come home.

"Perhaps if I talk to my uncle – "

She cut him off. "I talked to him. I told him I'd cut off his manhood if he ever touched me again. He went off in search of something to beat me with, or at least that's what I think he was shouting about. I don't know. That's when I left to come here."

"Right. All right." Mithra rubbed his face with his hands.

"It is most certainly NOT all right."

"No, but I don't know what else I can do. If you stay here, my parents would soon find out about you, which means the rest of the street would know within the week, and someone would sell you to the soldiers sooner than that. The only safe place for you is Seda's house. If you can stay away from my uncle…"

"He came to my bed!"

"Is there anywhere else you might sleep? Their house is much bigger than ours. Perhaps in the stables…"

Melisende wanted to slap him – if her father knew she had to sleep in a stable! – but her father wouldn't be pleased with her sleeping anywhere but her chamber at home. Grudgingly, she offered, "There is a hayloft above the stables which you can only reach by a ladder, which I could pull up after me. I doubt he'd find me there."

"Then that is what you must do. I'm sorry, Lady Melisende, that I cannot offer you better accommodations, but I am merely a woodcutter, and what you see here is how I live. If it were safe to enter any of the inns, I would take you to one at once, but the soldiers… the soldiers…I'm trying to keep you safe in the only way I can. If only the angels had sent you a better protector. One of their own, or a knight, maybe, but I am merely…me. Forgive me."

Now she regretted her outburst. What man in her village at home – let alone a woodcutter – would offer her such assistance, if they'd found her in the woods alone? He'd done nothing but help her, in any way he could. His uncle might be a piece of filth, but Mithra was a good man.

"There is nothing to forgive," she said. On a whim, she kissed his cheek. For a moment, she thought a spark had passed between them, but surely she had imagined it. "I will go, and ascend to my new hayloft bedchamber."

He took a deep breath. "If you wish, I could come with you, and stand guard while you sleep."

She'd never wanted a man in her bedchamber, but if she was to trust any man in it, it would be Mithra. "I would like – "

A thunderous hammering came from the front door. "Ali Baba, I know you are home! Open the door this instant!"

"It's him!" Mithra hissed. "I don't know what he's doing here, but if he finds you…Go, Melisende, go! I will keep him here for as long as I can, so that you are safe in your eyrie when he returns."

Once again, Melisende bolted, but more than once, she caught herself glancing behind to see if he was following.

No, not Kasim. Instead, she hoped for Mithra.

Thirty-One

By the time Mithra reached the front door, he found not only had his father opened it but Kasim had already bulled his way inside.

After feeling the full force of Melisende's fury, Mithra was more than ready to fight the man himself. His father knew nothing of Melisende, or what had transpired in Kasim's house tonight, so it seemed safest to be civil. To start with, at least.

"Good evening, Uncle," Mithra said. "Is there some urgent matter that you wish father's help with, that you must visit so late?"

Uncle Kasim's eyes narrowed. "Yes, most urgent. You did not seem to think so. We are family! I allow you to live in this house at so low a rent it is positively criminal, yet when the tables are turned, I find you are not willing to share your good fortune with me."

Mithra and his father exchanged confused glances. This had nothing to do with Melisende, so even Mithra had no idea what the man meant.

"My most esteemed brother," Ali Baba began. "Have you perhaps drunk a little too much wine? My wife has recently lost her position as Gatehouse cook, but I would hardly consider that good fortune."

Kasim's brows lowered until they almost met over his hawk-like nose. "Pah! What do I care about your wife or the pennies they pay her? Not when you possess gold so plentiful you did not even notice that these were missing!" He pulled something out of the pouch at his waist and tossed it at the table. The coins flew across the surface before tinkling to the floor.

Ali Baba bent to retrieve them. When he

raised his head above the table, his expression had turned from confusion to dread. Carefully, he laid the three gold coins on the table.

"Do not lie to me, brother. Your son dropped these at my house weeks ago, and only found them tonight. Where are the rest?" Kasim demanded.

Ali Baba closed his eyes. "I will show you." He rose.

Mithra was faster. "No. I shall. I found them in a cave in the forest when I was out cutting wood."

"Aha!" Kasim turned to his brother. "Did you think you could keep such wealth to yourself? Are we not brothers, who share everything?"

If Kasim's words were true, then he would have invited them to live with him in the Merchants' Quarter, instead of charging them what was actually quite a normal rate of rent for a cottage here.

"I'll take you now if you like," Mithra offered.

Kasim's eyes gleamed with even more greed than usual. "Not without bringing some beasts to carry the treasure home. What is to stop you from stealing it the moment I am gone and hiding it somewhere else? No, I shall take my share now. Wait right here, while I go get some horses."

Mithra started in panic. If Kasim went to his stables and found Melisende…

"No, not horses! What you want is mules. Sturdy beasts, who are used to carrying great weights. If you mean to carry your half of the treasure away with you, you will need as many mules as you can find."

Kasim nodded thoughtfully. "You see, brother? Your son knows the value of family, if you do not. Perhaps I shall make him my heir if my barren wife does not bother to give me a son."

Mithra had no desire for anything his uncle had touched, but he was not a fool, either. With or without the thieves' gold, inheriting his uncle's business at some point in the future could not be a bad thing.

"Thank you, Uncle. I will wait here while you get the mules."

Wearing a grin so wide he truly resembled

the toad Melisende had called him, Kasim dashed out into the darkness.

169

Thirty-Two

It was nearly noon by the time Mithra and his uncle reached the cave. They'd started out shortly after dawn, but Kasim had insisted upon far too many mules, all roped together. Even with Mithra at the front and Kasim bringing up the rear, the animals managed to tangle the ropes in trees more than a dozen times before they had travelled a mile.

Then his uncle started complaining about the heat, and the distance, followed by how ungrateful Mithra and his whole family were. At this point, Mithra was more than ready to leave his uncle in the woods to find his way out on his own.

But he was family, and there was more wealth in the cave than Mithra and his family could ever use, so he did not see a problem sharing it with his uncle.

Before they'd left, his father had warned him to be careful, and Mithra meant to be.

So when he finally reached the clearing and ascertained that it was empty, Mithra finally dared to breathe a sigh of relief.

"I don't see a cave. Where is this magical place?" Kasim complained.

Mithra merely walked over to the boulder and said, "Open sesame."

Just as before, the cavern opened.

"After you, Uncle," Mithra said with a bow.

For a moment, Kasim looked suspicious, before he peered down the steps. He must have caught the glitter of gold or something else that changed his mind, for he trotted down the first few steps, before turning to block Mithra's path.

"You stay up here and mind the mules," he said. "I shall choose what treasure to take as my share, and you may have the rest."

Mithra shrugged. If his father had his way, their share would be nothing at all, at least until they had run out of the gold he'd already brought home. Seeing as he hadn't spent anything yet, that could take quite some time.

Deciding that his uncle would probably be a while, and that the man would shout if he needed him, Mithra tied the lead mule's rope to a tree and found a suitable bush to shade him while he caught up on some much needed sleep.

Mithra woke some time later to angry shouts. At first he thought they'd come from his uncle, until he realised that he'd heard several voices shouting at once, and his uncle's was not one of them.

Carefully, Mithra rose up onto his knees and peered between the branches. His worst fears were realised — a large number of men occupied the clearing with the mules, and they were most unhappy at having to share.

"Look! Someone has moved the stone!" One thief pointed, but they all turned to look.

Mithra's heart sank. He had to warn his

uncle, but he didn't know how. He could not reach the cave without running through the thieves, who would surely kill him on sight. His only hope was that his uncle had heard them, and that he'd found somewhere inside the cave to hide until the thieves had left.

So Mithra held his breath, and waited. The thieves approach the cave entrance, their steps stealthy, and their swords drawn. Down the steps they went, two at a time, sealing the entrance behind them.

When Mithra was certain that all forty of them had gone in, only then did he dare move. He raced across the clearing, and climbed the tree where he and Melisende had sat when they'd first learned the secrets of the cave.

He waited and he waited, until finally, the boulder moved and the thieves emerged. Mithra counted forty men, with no sign of his uncle among them.

"That will serve as a lesson to anyone who thinks to steal from us," the leader said. "Untie the mules. We shall sell them to recover the cost of what has already been stolen from us."

His men took the mules and departed.

Mithra stayed in his tree, waiting until he was certain they had all gone. Then he waited a little more until the sun seemed ready to sink beneath the horizon. He wished he could go home, get his father and together they could find out what had happened to his uncle. But Mithra was a man, not a frightened child, which is what he knew his father would say. Besides, his uncle might still be alive.

With that heartening thought, Mithra told the stone to shift aside.

He descended into the gloom, allowing his eyes to adjust to the dim twilight as he called softly, "Uncle? Uncle Kasim? It's me, Mithra. They've gone, it's safe to come out." He waited a moment, then repeated the words, several times, but still he got no answer. He stepped off the bottom step and trod in something soft. Mithra glanced down, then recoiled in horror.

Beneath his boot was a hand that ended in a bloody stump where the wrist should be. Another hand lay several yards away, with two arms and a torso in pieces between them. The legs and feet were off to the right, while his uncle's head had rolled almost to the wall on his left.

Mithra fought not to lose what little he'd eaten that morning. He wasn't sure what he'd expected to find, but his uncle's dismembered body was not it.

What would he tell his father?

Or his aunt?

Not wanting to leave his uncle's remains there, Mithra bundled the pieces into a bale of cloth, wrapping the winding sheet around them until he was sure he had them all secure. Then he forced the grisly bundle into the biggest sack he could find, and began the long journey home.

Thirty-Three

When he finally reached home, it was past sunset and the lamps had been lit. Mithra paused at the door, trying to decide where to take his uncle's body. He caught the sound of feminine voices inside, and thanked whatever watchful angel had slowed his steps. If his mother had a visitor, he couldn't bring the body inside.

He laid the sack on his handcart instead, gathering up an armload of firewood to lay over it to conceal it.

"Mithra, is that you?" his father asked.

Shuffling footsteps sounded before his father was silhouetted in the doorway. "Where is Kasim? Seda arrived just before sundown, hysterical with worry that she hadn't seen him since he left last night. Your mother is trying to calm her down, for if Kasim were to see her like this…"

He would beat her, Mithra knew with a certainty he would not have possessed if it wasn't for Melisende's story last night. But his father had known.

Though he hated to even think it, Mithra suspected his uncle might have deserved his fate.

"Uncle Kasim is dead. Killed by the thieves, who happened upon us while Uncle was collecting treasure from the cave. I managed to hide, but Uncle…" He gestured toward the sack. "They chopped his body into pieces. I could not leave him there. What should I do now?"

Mithra had spent years learning the trade of both a merchant and a woodcutter, but neither had prepared him for a situation like this. Surely his father would know.

His father stood in thoughtful silence for a moment, then said, "You must take him home. Put his body in the cellar or somewhere cool, and see that he is laid out for his funeral. I will keep your aunt here for as long as I can, to give you time to do what you must. See that her maid has a sleeping draught ready for her when she arrives, if you need more time."

Melisende. Melisende would help, and hopefully know what to do. She'd been a healer. Did that mean she'd had to lay out bodies for funerals before? Because no healer could save everyone…

Mithra found himself nodding, lifting up the handles of his handcart to deliver Kasim home for the last time.

He trudged through the streets with his cart, forcing his voice to sound cheerful as he told every soldier he met how he was on his last firewood delivery of the night. None of them seemed to care, or feel the need to shift the thin layer of branches camouflaging Kasim's remains.

Mithra reached Kasim's door and knocked softly.

He knew the angels had answered his prayer when Melisende opened it.

Mithra's breath whooshed out of him in a great gust of relief. He'd never been so glad to see anyone in his life.

"Help me with this," he said, pushing the barrow toward the cellar entrance.

Hesitantly, Melisende followed.

"Close the door," he said, seizing the firewood and stacking it with the rest. That left only the sack on the handcart, which he could not seem to bring himself to open.

Melisende didn't share his qualms. She strode across the cellar and reached for the fastening. "What's in here?"

All his life, he'd been brought up to believe women should be sheltered, not subjected to a man's life of blood and toil. Especially highborn ones like her. His instincts screamed at him to be silent.

But if he didn't tell her, she'd find out for herself, and she deserved a warning before having Kasim's blood on her hands.

"It's Kasim. Hacked up into little pieces and bundled into a sack."

He waited for her to faint or scream or some such ladylike thing that Seda would definitely have done.

Melisende blinked. "That is…very kind of you, but you didn't need to kill him for me. Uh, thank you, I suppose. I only threatened to cut off his manhood. Not…everything. But if this is how such things are done here, I guess I should be grateful. At home, this would be considered murder and you'd be in trouble for it. Are things so different out here in the desert?"

Mithra's breath caught in his throat. She thought he'd brought his uncle's body as a gift? A laugh burst out of him, the sound startling her as much as him.

It took him a moment to get himself under control enough to speak. "I didn't kill him. The Forty Thieves did. You see…" Mithra spilled out the whole story, not leaving out anything, including his own cowardice.

Melisende's eyes widened. "They'll come here next. If what you said is true, they'll find out who he is and come after his family. We'll have to hide his death long enough to make it look like something else. Some sort of sickness, maybe, so no one suspects…but Seda is still out looking for him. I'll tell her…I found him in the cellar, unconscious and wounded, after he fell down the stairs, and that I've made up a sickbed for him there, so that I might tend to his wounds. Infection that proceeds to necrosis…I'll go to the apothecary for medicine in the morning, and keep returning to say he is worse until…well, until the blood poisoning could reasonably kill him. Fastest would be a gut wound, which would take less than a week. Hence the need to mention necrosis and a wound, to account for the smell at the funeral." She gave a little nod. "That should work."

Mithra could not help staring. "You thought all that up right then?"

Melisende shrugged. "Mostly. It's only a rough plan. It will surely need more thought if it's to work. Would your family visit if your uncle is sick?" At his nod, she continued, "Then you must definitely visit every day, and see that everyone you meet knows of Kasim's illness. You say your father knows, so only you and he should come down to the cellar to see Kasim. I will try to stitch the body together as best I can, then cover it with a sheet, so that at least to anyone who looks into the cellar, he will appear to be a sick man instead of a dead one. And buy some herbs to burn to cover the smell..."

Mithra nodded, trying to commit all the details to memory, so that he might help her in any way he could. He didn't know what he'd do without her.

Thirty-Four

Melisende was surprised at how smoothly her plan went. She'd dealt with one or two cases like the one she'd described to Mithra, so it was easy to state the right symptoms to the apothecary.

She'd stitched the mostly bloodless body together, then bandaged it tightly and bundled it into some of Kasim's clothes. The bloodied rags and sack Mithra had brought the body in were burned with some of Mithra's firewood, leaving no sign of what had really happened to Kasim.

Dealing with Seda was another matter. At first, she'd insisted on seeing her husband, saying it was her duty as a good wife, but she'd gagged at the smell from the stairs and scuttled out again. By the end of the day, Melisende had her convinced that sending her maid to nurse the man was more than anyone would expect of a good wife. Perhaps if Kasim had been a better husband, or done something to deserve his wife's love, it might not have been so easy, but as it was…

Mithra and his family came every day, spending long hours with Seda. Mithra escaped to find Melisende as often as he dared, meeting her in the stables so they could get away from the ghastly smell in the cellar. Melisende brought a selection of food from the kitchen, which they shared, while they told each other tales about their lives before the crusade.

For the first time in her life, she told someone what it felt like to use her magic to run with horses or to travel swiftly when someone's life depended on it. For Mithra had seen how fast she could run, when she'd used her momentum against him, and there was no point in pretending it was a secret between them.

He in turn told her about Peter and Simon and the family he'd spent his apprenticeship with. Several times, he'd started to say how much she'd like Peter, but stopped himself. Then, a shadow would pass across his face before he changed the subject.

Melisende had wanted to hug him, each and every time, but if Mithra was anything like her brothers, he'd only push her and her girlish sentimentality away. Then again, none of her brothers had ever lost their best friend in what Mithra said had been a particularly brutal murder.

But their idyll soon came to an end, when Melisende had to go to the apothecary to buy a sleeping draught to help calm Kasim's newly widowed wife.

Seda was not allowed to attend her own husband's funeral, Melisende learned, for that was a men's affair alone. Mithra and Ali Baba had stayed for long enough to leave Mithra's mother, Banu, to comfort the grieving widow, before they departed with Kasim's coffin.

Then the women, Seda's friends, started to arrive.

Melisende was run off her feet, fetching things from the kitchen to feed the hungry hordes. Banu — a cook herself, if Melisende remembered Mithra's words correctly — worked alongside the cook, issuing a stream of orders that Melisende hurried to obey. She hadn't worked this hard since the last Yule feast at home when her mother was still alive.

But when the day was done and Melisende thought she might be able to creep up to bed, the cook sent her to clean out Kasim's bedchamber, and another across the passage that was reserved for guests, if Kasim had ever had any.

"Why?" Melisende asked crossly.

"Because tomorrow, Kasim's heir moves into his new house, and the family's rooms must be clean, or they will dismiss you as a bad servant," the cook said.

If they did that, they'd deserve whatever retribution the Forty Thieves visited upon them, Melisende thought. But then her sluggish mind turned up another thought that wouldn't go away. "But Seda is his widow. Isn't the house hers?"

She'd heard Seda say something about how she'd grown up in this house, which had belonged to her father.

"Of course not. She couldn't inherit, but her father had no sons, so he willed it to her husband instead. When Kasim died, everything he owned passed to his nearest male heir. Luckily for her, he's a kind man, who will let her stay."

"Who is he?" Melisende asked. If he was anywhere near as bad as Kasim, she wanted to be warned.

"Ali Baba."

Mithra's father. Which meant…

"Mithra's moving in here?" Melisende blurted out.

"That's the young master to you, girl. He'll be taking over his uncle's shop and all the rest of the business, so Master Mithra will be a much more important man. He won't be a woodcutter any more." The cook headed off, with a satisfied air as if she expected her orders to be obeyed.

Melisende smiled. Master Mithra. Merchant Mithra. She knew how much he longed to be able to practice his trade again, and tomorrow he would finally achieve his dream. It was fitting that he slept in a fine bed in his uncle's best room.

And she was in a position to provide it.

Suddenly possessed of a new burst of energy, Melisende set to work.

Tomorrow was going to be a good day.

Thirty-Five

Mithra arrived at Kasim's shop well before dawn, hoping to have time to go over the books and stock before opening the shop at the normal time later on that morning. Yet when he opened the door and raised his lantern to look inside, Mithra had to remind himself that it was not his uncle's shop any more. It was his, his father had told him, and his alone. His father had expressed hope that Simon's teachings during Mithra's long apprenticeship would stand him in good stead to keep the shop as profitable as it had been under his uncle's aegis.

Mithra hoped so too.

Yet as he lit the lamps – far too few, in his opinion – he did not feel the same confidence he had in Simon's shop. This place looked dim and dingy, which meant the goods could not catch a buyer's eye as easily as if they were brightly lit.

Mithra shook his head. Never mind the lights. He could make changes on the morrow, when he had a day's trade under his belt which he could then compare to the next day's takings, to see if there had been any improvement. As Simon had often said, the numbers did not lie.

But first, he had to find the numbers, and Kasim's books could be anywhere.

After an hour of looking, Mithra began to despair of ever finding Kasim's records in the cluttered shop. But when he turned too swiftly and tipped over a pile of brass bells that seem to want to roll everywhere, he found a dusty bookshelf tucked under a table which contained records dating back to before Seda's father's time. Selecting the most recent volume, Mithra sat down and began to read.

It took Mithra several hours to determine with any certainty how bad a businessman his uncle had been, by which time he knew he'd need to read all the records, to work out just how much mess the shop was in.

Mithra did not open the shop on the first day, nor the second. In fact, it was almost a full week before he dared to open the awning and allow people inside.

He needn't have bothered. No one seemed to want to enter the dark space, and those who looked like they might consider it were chased away by the surly looks of the man who owned the shop next door. The same man who had accused Mithra of being a thief, when he tried to buy clothes from the man. Mithra began to realise why his uncle's business had been doing so badly.

That had to change, he resolved. Kasim's shop had plenty of stock, but it was piled up haphazardly in such a way that no one could find what they wanted. Mithra had looked in vain for any record of Kasim's warehouse, where some of this clutter might be stored, only to find that he had sold it more than a year ago, to some Crusader merchant who likely had no use for it now.

Mithra had lost count of the number of times he'd wished he were back in Simon's well-lit, well-laid-out shop, in its prime place in the market. Mithra had no doubt if he got some of Kasim's goods to Simon's shop, they would sell so much better. In fact...

Mithra took a fresh piece of parchment and began to take stock. If he used this place as his warehouse, and opened up Simon's shop, Mithra might be able to actually sell something.

Simon had owned his shop, and still no one seemed to have tried to take possession of it, so Mithra decided to try his luck.

Before dawn the next day, he began moving a selection of stock that he thought might capture soldiers' eyes into Simon's shop. He was still arranging his wares when the other shops around him began to open, and more than one soldier had taken advantage of the open awning to come and ask Mithra if he would be opening for business again.

And then came the magic words.

"Because I was hoping you might have…"

A customer who told him exactly what he wanted was the easiest sale a merchant could make, Mithra knew.

And that afternoon, he opened.

By the time he closed, he had sold out of several items, including those benighted brass bells, and he lingered a little longer in the market to bring another shipment from Kasim's shop to Simon's.

The next day, he did more business in a day than Kasim had in his last month.

Not that he could celebrate yet. His numbers told him that he'd only achieved an average sales day for Simon's shop, with its superior position and all. He could do better than this.

After several days, setting up the shop differently every morning, and filling it with new stock every night, Mithra made a new record.

For the first time, he sold more goods in a day than Simon's shop had ever sold since the start of his apprenticeship. If there had been a merchants' guild in Dorylaeum, they might have awarded him mastery on the spot. As it was, Mithra found himself trying out a new name in his head, testing out how it felt.

Master Mithra. Master Merchant Mithra.

He laughed to himself. Never in his wildest dreams had he imagined this would be possible for him.

Something he could thank his uncle for…

No. This was Melisende's doing. If she had not arrived, and shown him the thieves' cave, Kasim would be still alive, slowly running his own shop down into bankruptcy.

He owed her everything. And yet she still served as a maid in his uncle's house, waiting for the army to leave so that she might go home.

He shook his head. Melisende had not said a word of complaint, which surely made her an angel – his guardian angel, if such things existed. He could not give her the object of her desire just yet, but he owed her at least a gift, as a token of thanks for all she had done.

He scanned the marketplace, trying to find something suitable. This was made near impossible by the fact that most of the shops, like his own, had pulled their awnings down and closed for the night.

But some lanterns were still lit, including the one at the bakery where Cagri worked.

She stood at the counter, serving supper to a long line of customers, while the smell of yeast from the back room told him that the bread for tomorrow was already rising.

"So how can I help you?" Cagri asked, fluttering those eyelashes that used to send his heart fluttering, too.

But he saw no light of recognition in her eyes, and her words were hollow, when he knew that she said the same thing and looked the same way at any prosperous young man who entered her shop. How could he have ever thought her beautiful? Or imagined that he loved her?

He'd been such a fool.

And then he'd met Melisende…

The Crusader maiden who had never heard of sesame before, or tasted a cake made of the stuff.

"Do you have any sesame cakes left?" Mithra asked.

They only had one, and a small one at that.

When Cagri read the disappointment in his eyes, she offered all manner of other things instead, including a delivery of a whole box of cakes upon the morrow, if he wished.

No. One was enough. He would give it to Melisende, and watch her expression as she ate it. Most likely, she would hate it, for Peter's sisters had not been fond of them, he recalled. They did not like the seeds that caught in their teeth, or some other such silliness.

It mattered not. He would keep his promise to Melisende, and tell her how grateful he was for all of her assistance. They lived under the same roof, yet he had not seen her since his uncle's funeral, and that had been weeks ago.

He paid for his purchase, and headed out into the night. And if there was a spring in his step in anticipation of seeing her again, Mithra did not mind at all.

Thirty-Six

"What of the maid? She's lasted longer than most of them, and she seems a willing enough worker."

Melisende had been about to enter the kitchen, but at the sound of Mithra's mother's voice, she waited a moment. She needed to hear this.

The cook spoke next. "She works, yes, but she's not like any of the others we had before. This one has Crusader blood in her. Some Crusader's bastard, I'd wager, who'd never worked a day in her life before she came here.

You wouldn't believe the things I had to show her how to do!"

Only because the cook wanted everything done in such a particular way, no one would have known what she wanted before she told them, Melisende fumed. She'd scolded Melisende for boiling water wrong. When Melisende had bottled more potions than this woman had made meals, despite being half her age. If it weren't for Mithra, she would have left this place a long time ago. Oh, and the army. If they'd left. Yes, that's what she'd meant.

"Seda said she's the best maid she's ever had. She's helped her with her hair and gown more than any of the other girls. Like she was a lady's maid or something before. Maybe to some Crusader lady…"

"If she's lost one position in a fine house, you can be sure she's got her eye out for another one. Lady of this one, perhaps. You should find your son a wife as soon as possible, Banu. Before she seduces him. You know Crusader girls are neither modest or obedient. If I had a coin for every insolent look that girl has given me, I would be rich enough to pay someone to cook for me!"

Incredulous, not insolent. Melisende shook her head. Never mind. It wasn't like she needed a herbal infusion to help her sleep. She was tired enough most nights as it was.

Tonight was no different. She'd barely laid her head upon her pillow and she was asleep.

What felt like less than a moment later, she awoke again, to the sound of footsteps outside her room. Kasim was dead and buried, she told herself, as she rose as silently as she could and crept to the wall, where she'd hung up her clothes and her knife.

"Melisende? Are you in here?"

She let the sheathed knife fall. Mithra was hardly a threat. "Give me a moment to dress," she called, tugging a gown over her shift. At home, she'd have needed to lace up the gown, but the shapeless garments that were the fashion here had no lacings at all. Probably a good thing, for she suspected Mithra would not know how to help her lace a gown.

She stepped out into the passage, which was lit by a lantern at Mithra's feet. He must have just arrived home from his shop, because she'd filled every lamp in the house more times than she could count, and that lantern wasn't one of them.

"What do you need?" she asked briskly. At this late hour, it had to be something urgent.

"I need…to thank you. For everything you've done that's changed my fortunes so much I can scarcely believe it's possible."

"You woke me up…to thank me?"

"I didn't realise you'd be asleep so early. Or maybe I just didn't realise how late it was. I've been working so many hours in the shop…"

Melisende felt a rush of sympathy for him. It wasn't all that long ago that she'd struggled to learn a whole new occupation, and her body still hadn't adjusted to the workload. She summoned a smile as she took his hand. "Come, I'll make you a healing draught that will help you sleep, so you'll be well-rested in the morning."

"In the kitchen?" He didn't sound particularly eager to accept her offer.

"Of course." For all the size of this house and its outbuildings, there was no stillroom, so the kitchen it must be.

"Just that my mother and the cook are talking about finding me a wife, and comparing the various virtues of all the local girls. If I go in there…"

Suddenly, this shadowy hallway seemed the best place to be.

"I don't need anything, anyway. I had my supper at the shop, while I was doing the day's figures. Then, I decided it was time to celebrate, and I realised I had a promise to keep."

To take her home. That had been weeks ago, and the army still showed no sign of leaving. Maybe she'd be a housemaid forever.

Melisende shook her head. "I can't expect you to work miracles, Mithra. Without your help, I wouldn't have been safe for all these weeks. You found me food and lodging…" Even if she did have to work for it, she thought but didn't say. It wasn't his fault he hadn't been born in a castle or grand house, with rooms to spare for as many guests as he liked. Well, now his father's house had that, but the soldiers still marched through the streets, so she could hardly proclaim her true identity yet.

"Yes! Food! I finally remembered to get you a sesame cake!"

He held out something round, roughly the size of his palm.

Now she needed her knife to cut a cake. Melisende wanted to laugh, but one look at his earnest expression and she didn't dare.

Instead, she gingerly took the cake from him and bit into it. A cloyingly sweet, sticky mass hit her tongue. A mass that proved surprisingly chewy, despite the gritty seeds that gave the cake its name. Finally, she managed to swallow.

"What did you think?" he asked eagerly.

"It's…good?" she managed to say. She ventured another bite. If anything, this time it tasted even sweeter, coating her mouth in stickiness. She'd need a drink after this. Would Mithra be offended if she went to draw a bucket of water from the well?

"Here." As if guessing her thoughts, he held out his water bottle.

Taking the leather flask in her free hand, she

drank deeply before trying to hand it back.

He waved it away. "Keep it until you're done. Peter's father used to buy us each one on special feast days. When I tried my first one, I stuck my head in the water barrel. Peter laughed so hard he spat cake everywhere."

She held out what remained of the cake. "Then you should have some. Truly, I cannot eat another bite."

She washed her hands while he finished it off.

"Peter would have loved to meet you," he said.

"I can't imagine what it must be like, to have so many memories of someone, and then to have them plucked from your life, as if they'd never existed," Melisende said. She leaned in to kiss his cheek. "Thank you for sharing this with me."

Maybe it was dark, or maybe she'd misjudged. Or maybe he'd turned his head at just the wrong moment, and that's why she missed.

But the moment her mouth met his, time stopped.

And it was more magical than anything she'd ever done in her life.

Until his lips left hers.

Only then did she realise that time had not stopped, though it had felt like it.

Somehow, she'd twined her arms around his neck, and wound her legs around his waist. His hard body pinned her back to the wall, holding her up, while his hands were busy elsewhere. When he'd tangled his fingers in her hair, somehow her braid had come undone, the way the rest of her body wanted to. His other hand cupped her face as tenderly as if she was his most treasured possession. The look in his eyes said he wanted her to be.

Then he set her down and stepped away, hanging his head. "Forgive me, Lady Melisende. I forgot myself. For a moment, I thought I was better than I am. But it seems I am no better than my uncle, stealing what was never mine to take. Maybe I deserve the same fate."

He turned on his heel and was gone.

Melisende's knees did not have the strength to hold her, so she slid down the wall to sit on the floor instead. Her lips burned from his kiss, a kiss sweeter than any cake, which made her hunger for all manner of forbidden things.

"Oh, Mithra. You can't steal a kiss when it's freely given. And after that, you have only to ask, and I would give you a million more." Much more.

She squeezed her eyes shut. The cook was right, though Melisende had not known it until now. She did want to seduce Mithra.

If the army did not depart soon, allowing her to leave, she'd do it, too. For she knew she could not resist him.

She laughed softly to herself. All her life, she'd laughed at the girls who flirted, trying to win the attention of whatever man they fancied. All it took was one kiss to turn her into the worst of them all.

Reluctantly, she returned to her bed, expecting sleep to elude her. Instead, she fell instantly into a dream where Mithra returned with more kisses and caresses.

When she woke the next morning, no amount of water could cool her burning blushes.

Thirty-Seven

On the morrow, Mithra threw himself into his work once more. When he went to Rialto, he would offer to purchase Simon's shop from his family, and that would take more gold than he currently had. Unless he used the coins he'd taken from the thieves' cave…

No. To do that would be to draw attention to the fact that someone other than Kasim knew the thieves' secret, and they would come after him and his family.

And Melisende…

Mithra buried his face in his hands at the

thought of her. He'd come to her chamber last night to thank her, to give her a gift and tell her he had not forgotten his promise to help her.

Instead, he'd behaved no better than his uncle, pinning her against the wall so that she could not escape while his mouth plundered hers, stealing kisses he did not deserve.

She'd been so frozen with fear she hadn't even tried to fight back. He was as bad as his uncle, no better than the soldiers who'd stolen all those Crusader girls and used them for their own sordid pleasure. Why, he'd forced this highborn lady into servitude. She cooked and scrubbed floors when he was the one who should be fetching things for her, serving her…

He was a fool. While he might be a merchant now, he would not remain one for long if he didn't buy more goods to trade. He'd go back to being a penniless woodcutter, what he would always, always be. No match for a Crusader lady.

He couldn't even meet his mother's eyes, knowing she wanted him to wed, when the only woman he wanted was one he could not have.

So he worked, and he worked, and one day he went back out the army camp and asked to see the General. He offered to buy all the remaining goods in the Crusaders' warehouses, and the General agreed.

He sold Kasim's shop to the clothes merchant, shifted what little stock that remained to Simon's shop, and set off for the Warehouse District. While he found many warehouses – Simon's included, sadly – that had been plundered of everything they contained, others, like the one Kasim had sold, were relatively untouched, and they contained a wealth far beyond what he'd paid to the General.

Now he had an excuse not to return to the house until very late at night, leaving early every morning, consolidating all his trade goods in the warehouses with the stoutest doors, while he decided what to sell here and what to ship off to other markets, when the army left. And they would. They had to, for, faithless wretch that he was, he owed it to

Melisende to take her home, like he'd promised. Then, and only then, would she be safe from him.

Thirty-Eight

"Excuse me, but are you Master Mithra?" a little boy asked.

Mithra looked up from his books. The urchin could have been him at that age.

"I am," Mithra said.

"Got a message for you, Master. Your father says to come home quick, because there's someone to see you. Some merchant from far away looking to trade. Says he did business with your uncle."

One of Kasim's business contacts. The first he'd heard of, as Kasim hadn't kept records of who had sold him things. His father was right – he needed to meet this man.

"Thank you," he told the boy, tossing him a coin.

The boy had bolted out of sight by the time Mithra made it out into the street, but it didn't matter. He knew the way home.

The house was a blaze of lights – even the stables had the lanterns lit, and he could hear horses inside it for the first time in as long as he could remember. He stuck his head inside and exchanged nods with the two men tending the horses. He recognised them both as grooms who worked at one of the city's inns. Well, they had worked there – maybe they'd lost their jobs like his mother had.

It appeared they had a new job now – more horses than Mithra thought would fit in this stable, but then he was no expert when it came to animals. Trees and trade were where his talents lay. And trade was what he wanted.

He headed up to the house, where his father was no doubt entertaining their mysterious merchant guest in the dining chamber.

Outside the door, he paused to listen to

their conversation.

"You would not believe it, but we were a day's ride from anywhere, and out of the desert marched a line of mules, all roped together! I stepped up to take the lead animal's halter, and they all just stopped. I let out a shout to tell everyone they were safe and it was not a company of soldiers come to kill us all, and we soon had the fire lit again, with dinner back on the spit. I knew a horse dealer here in town, so I brought them to him today, hoping they'd fetch a fair price. But you know horse dealers – he tried to offer me far too little. So I said I'd sell them to my friend Kasim, a merchant I know who always needs more mules, and he'll give me a fair price. He always has in the past…"

There was no mention of any mules in Kasim's books, Mithra knew, for he'd been through them twice. Not even the mules he'd purchased on the day he died. Whoever this merchant was, he must be mistaken.

"So he said he'd take another look at them, and when he did, he said these were Kasim's mules, for he'd sold them to him just last week!"

Unless Kasim's ghost had been buying mules, someone was lying. Likely the horse dealer, for Mithra knew Simon had had bad dealings with him in the past.

Approaching footsteps made him turn. It was just the cook, bringing a tray of food.

Best that she didn't catch him lurking out here. Mithra entered the room.

Father introduced his son to the merchant, "Judah of Kerioth, a Christian," or so Ali Baba said.

The man certainly dressed like a Crusader, but his name seemed familiar, while the man himself did not. Perhaps Simon or his uncle had mentioned him.

Mithra accepted a cup of wine, watching as the cook refilled the merchant's cup. He drank far more than Father, and seemed to be sweating excessively in the heat.

"A Christian in Dorylaeum! It has been some months since we've seen one. Please, tell me your secret. How did you manage to evade the Seljuk army?" Mithra asked.

For if this man could, then he could take

Melisende home.

"What Seljuk army? I saw no such thing, though we had heard they were about. We had a terrible fright one night when a pack of mules came upon us in the dark. You will not believe me…" The merchant began his tale again.

Mithra considered stopping him, but instead he let his thoughts drift. Let the man get comfortable, and enjoy their house's hospitality. A well-fed man would be well disposed to trade with Mithra, and for a favourable price. For whatever this merchant dealt in, if Mithra could find a way to sell it, he wanted to buy it all. At the best price, of course.

On the morrow, when their deal was concluded, then he could tell Melisende the good news and begin planning their journey.

Thirty-Nine

"Two of the lamps have gone out. Go and refill them all," the cook commanded, coming back to the kitchen with an empty tray.

Melisende bit back a curse. "I can't. I used the last of the lamp oil to fill the lamps in the guest chamber I've just finished preparing for the master's visitor."

The cook's oath was not as quiet as Melisende's. Then her eyes lit up. "The man's an oil merchant. He won't mind if you take some from one of his jars — there were dozens of them!"

Melisende frowned. "Stealing from a guest goes against the laws of hospitality." Though she knew her culture and the cook's were very different, the laws of hospitality were universal.

The cook waved away her worries. "Not when the guest intends to sell that oil to the master. They'll bargain about the price over dinner, but by morning, those jars will belong to the master. Why else would he have brought them here, instead of to an inn or his own warehouse?"

Melisende had no answer for her, so she grabbed a jug and headed out to the stables. She'd been tempted to offer to take care of the guest's horses herself and tell the cook to hire a maid for the night, instead of grooms, but airing and washing linens was infinitely more preferable than shovelling horse shit, which was what the grooms would be doing come morning. So she'd held her tongue and nodded meekly, which had earned her a suspicious glance from the cook, but she'd managed the spring cleaning in her father's castle often enough to prepare a room on her own.

Then, as now, her thoughts had wandered

when doing such menial work, and today they'd flown outside the city gates, where this travelling merchant had come from. A Christian, the cook had said, which meant the army must be gone, or he'd found a way to sneak around them. Either way, it would be a simple matter for her to bundle up her meagre belongings and take the same route away from Dorylaeum. She could go home…

But not before she'd had a chance to bid farewell to Mithra. He usually returned home late, long after she'd retired for the night, so she hadn't seen him since the night they'd kissed, but tonight she'd wait. Besides, she had lamps to fill and who knew what other chores to keep her busy for a while.

She swung open the stable door, marvelling at the bustle of activity in the echoing, empty space where she and Mithra had taken refuge during Kasim's imaginary illness. Horses occupied every stall, plus anywhere they'd found space to tether the extra beasts once the stalls were full. There was no sign of any oil, or a vessel which might contain the stuff.

Maybe in the tackroom, Melisende thought

as she pushed open the door.

"Don't do that, miss, for the zebani in there will surely trample you to death!" a groom said, thrusting an arm between her and the open doorway.

Melisende glimpsed a set of flying hooves, which made a thunderous clatter as they hit the floor.

"See, miss? A creature come straight from hell itself!"

Surely not.

Silver destriers were rare, and if they'd been closer to home, Melisende would have wagered every coin she had that this fearsome animal had come from her father's stable. The horse reared again, and she was certain of it.

"Moonlight?" she called softly.

The gelding's ears pricked. Down went the hooves, and he lifted his nose to blow warm air across her outstretched hand. She waited a moment, then patted the horse's flank as her gaze swept the room. No oil jars here, either.

Something was amiss. Melisende just knew it.

"Are all the horses like this one?" she asked.

"No, miss, most are nice and calm. Happy to get something to eat. That one turns his nose up at everything and tries to trample anyone who approaches him. It's a wonder he let you near him."

Not a wonder at all, when you knew Moonlight and his twin brother Moonfire had learned to run alongside Melisende in the fields behind her father's castle. No, the wonder was how an oil merchant could afford a mount like Moonlight.

"Show me the other horses," she commanded.

The groom eyed her askance for a moment, before his shoulders drooped and he headed toward the stalls. "They're all just horses, miss."

It was true, and yet it wasn't. Melisende knew more about northern horse stock than most men alive, and these were no common horses. Palfreys, most of them, with a couple more destriers, along with a handful she thought might be packhorses. In the last stall, she had another surprise — a pale horse that could have been Moonlight's twin, at first glance, but this one was younger. Likely born during that long, cold winter when the snow had stayed on the ground well into spring, and the mares had kept warm by letting the stallions cover them. How many colts had been born that spring? Three, four? All named for the weather that year. "Snow? Sleet?" she tried. "Ice?" Then it came to her. "Frost!"

The palfrey lifted his head over the stall door, ears pricked. Melisende rushed to stroke him, too.

No mere merchant could afford two of her father's horses. Why, even Mithra, with all the gold in the thieves' cave, might not have enough for two of them.

These horses had belonged to knights, or princes, or noblemen with plenty of gold to spare. Men who had likely died on that battlefield. These were Crusaders' horses, all of them. Had this merchant bought them from the Seljuk army?

But no. The army hadn't taken the horses — they'd already been stolen by the Forty Thieves.

Thieves would sell to a Christian merchant,

Melisende told herself, but even that felt wrong. Surely thieves would know better than to sell horses of this calibre to be used as pack animals.

She'd think on it later, while she filled the lamps. Meanwhile, she still needed to find the oil.

"Where are the oil jars these horses were carrying?" she asked, half expecting the groom to deny any knowledge of them. After all, these horses didn't look like they'd been carrying heavy loads for many miles. They didn't look like they'd carried anything heavy at all.

"We put those in the cellar," the groom said. He led her to the yard and pointed. "Over there."

The cellar where Kasim's body had lain during his imaginary illness, which still smelled faintly of corruption. Of course.

She thanked the groom, and marched toward the cellar. When she threw the doors open, she saw a curious sight. The promised oil jars were lined up along the walls, much like the golden statues in the thieves' cave. A jug hung from the neck of each, swaying a little in the air flow from the open door.

She examined the first jug critically. It was made of cheap, thin clay, easily broken but able to hold a large quantity of oil. Suitable for lowering into the jar to scoop out a measure of oil, then pour it into her own sturdier vessel.

She unfasted the lid so that she might lower the jug inside.

"Is it time yet?"

She almost jumped out of her skin as the voice seemed to come from nowhere. No, from inside the jar!

"Because we've been talking, Captain. Does this thief have any daughters, or a comely young wife or two? It doesn't seem right to kill them all and burn down the house when we might take the women with us to enjoy later…"

Murmurs of assent came from the other jars.

The Forty Thieves had not sold the horses. They were here!

And if she didn't do something, they meant to leap from their jars and slaughter Mithra and his family before burning this place to the ground. Not to mention what they might do to her.

Her mind whirling with panic, she knew what she needed was time. Time to think, to get help, to decide what to do.

So she lifted up her jug, speaking into it to make her voice deep enough to pass for a man's as she said, "We shall see. The house is heavily guarded, so we must wait until they are all asleep or the guards will stop us. Wait for my signal, and I'll see you get the woman you deserve."

None, if she had any say in it, Melisende said to herself.

"When I tap on your jar, three times, tap back, so I know you understand," she added.

She walked along the row of jars, tapping on them and hearing her signal echoed back from every one except the last. She tapped again, but no sound came from it. Annoyed, she kicked the jar, only to hear the slosh of liquid inside.

So there was some oil, after all.

Melisende lifted off the lid and peered inside. An impossible idea kindled in her mind.

Forty

All the jugs sat on the table, brimful of oil and stoppered with a piece of rag that extended upward like a wisp of smoke. Smoke that would soon become flame.

She took a deep breath. This was her last chance to back out, to change her plan and go summon the guards. To find enough people to keep the thieves from killing Mithra and his family.

But if she left…the thieves might emerge early, and begin their terrible task.

These men had no mercy. She'd seen that

when they killed the Horn Knight. They'd slaughter Mithra and take her as their plaything.

No, she had to do this. She had no choice, for she was no man's toy.

She took a torch from the wall and waved it across the tops of the jugs. One, two, then a dozen rags caught alight. She would need to be swift and sure, so fast that she'd finished before the first man had time to react.

Melisende tugged on a pair of heavy leather gloves, hoping they would protect her. Even if they didn't…better burned hands than these men getting their hands on her body.

She bit down hard on her lip, tasting magic as time slowed.

Melisende seized an armload of jugs and raced along the jars. Lift the lid, throw the jug in so that it smashed, spilling flaming oil onto the man inside, then on to the next one.

More jugs. More lids. More breaking clay.

Again, and again.

Until there were no jugs left.

Melisende slumped against the table, reeling while she waited for the world to catch up to what she'd done.

And then the men began to scream.

She fled through the cellar door, barring it behind her before the horrible sounds reached the stables. She hoped no one in the house above heard.

Finally, the cellar fell silent. Melisende counted to a hundred, then did it again, before daring to open the door.

Nothing moved.

She crept down the steps, wrinkling her nose at what smelled like burned bacon.

By all that was holy…did cooked human flesh smell like bacon? No wonder Mithra's family never ate pork.

The smell only strengthened as she ventured deeper into the cellar, ably assisted by the fact that some of the jars were still smouldering.

Glad of the leather gloves she still wore, she set her hands on the rim of the nearest jar and peered inside.

Smoke stung her eyes, but the man inside didn't move. Nor did the next, or the next. She went around the whole room, checking until she was sure each jar held a corpse.

Only then did she dare to breathe again. The Forty Thieves were dead, and Mithra was safe.

Melisende swallowed. She'd killed forty men. Burned them alive. Her, the coward who'd run from the battlefield. She wished she could run now, run home and hide from this horrible thing she'd done.

Instead, she crawled into a corner and cried.

Moments passed, or maybe it was hours. She wasn't sure. What she did know was that she had no tears left. Not for the men she'd burned alive, or for the innocent girl she'd been before she'd slaughtered forty men.

But was it forty? Surely there'd been a sentry of some sort, and the captain they waited for.

Melisende counted the jars. "Thirty-eight, thirty-nine, forty." Yes, she had killed forty men.

She counted the jars again. But this time, when she got to the last one, she peered into inky blackness, for it was still mostly full of oil.

She'd killed thirty-nine of the Forty Thieves. Men who'd sworn vengeance on Mithra's family. If the last one found out what she'd done…

It must be their captain, for that's who they'd expected to come for them. Their captain must be the merchant, sharing a meal with Mithra's father even now, before he'd retire to the guest chamber beside Mithra's room. Mithra, who worked so hard and slept so soundly he wouldn't know there was an assassin in his chamber until the thief struck.

Numbly, Melisende drew a final jug of oil. She ascended the steps, jug held high, as she headed back to the house.

She'd killed thirty-nine men this night. What was one more?

Forty-One

Mithra almost choked on his wine when Melisende walked in with a tray of sweets. Judah's gaze was drawn to her, and she seemed to have eyes only for the merchant, too.

He was one of her people, Mithra told himself. The first she'd seen in weeks. Of course she'd stare, because she knew what the man's presence meant as much as Mithra did: the army was gone, and she could go home.

She served his father first, and then himself, despite Mithra's frantic gestures to serve their guest. Did she not know the most basic parts of the rules of hospitality?

It seemed she did not. Next, she set her tray down and refilled their wine cups, once again neglecting Judah.

"Serve our guest, girl," Ali Baba hissed.

Melisende moved around the table, snatched up a bowl and held it out to Judah.

Except, something seemed to go wrong. She tripped, or the bowl slipped, and instead of being set on the table before the man, it flew out of her hands and smacked into his chest, dribbling its contents down his tunic before clattering to the floor.

Melisende uttered a muffled curse, then dropped to her knees to clean up the mess with a cloth.

Judah glared down at her in fury.

"You must forgive our new maid, Master Judah," Mithra said with a forced smile. "She is still in training, and only just beginning to learn how to serve at table. I'll send her back to the kitchen and..."

Melisende had started to clean the man's tunic, dabbing at it with her cloth while muttering apologies.

Judah clouted her across the head. "Do not touch me, girl!" He lifted his head to meet Mithra's gaze. "Send the clumsy slut away. Ruining such costly silk. If she were my servant, I'd see her whipped –"

A line of red appeared across the merchant's throat, a line that began to rain, sheeting down his front and his already ruined tunic. His sentence ended in a choking sound as he pitched forward onto his plate.

While his father gaped, Mithra's mind worked faster. "Melisende, how could you do such a thing to a guest? Have you never heard of the laws of hospitality? We shall be cursed forever for this!"

Melisende rose gracefully to her feet and tossed a bloodied knife onto the table. The red jewels set in the gold hilt seemed to remind him of the hellish fires that surely awaited them all.

"That man's no guest. He hasn't eaten or drunk a thing, the whole time he's been here. Instead, he's been throwing it all on the floor beneath the table – see?" She lifted the cloth to reveal the mess Judah had made.

"Perhaps the man is a messy eater. But that's no reason to kill him!" Mithra said.

"He was clutching that dagger down by his side, under the table. I've seen it before — it was in my bag, and I left it in the thieves' cave. He dropped it when I threw his food at him, and he hit me when I picked it up. He's no merchant, and I'd wager he's no Christian, either. That tunic belonged to a knight I knew, who his men killed before dumping his body on the battlefield. This man is the captain of the Forty Thieves. He came here with his men to kill you all, and burn your house down. If anyone has broken all the laws of hospitality, it's him!" Fire blazed in her eyes. "If you don't believe me, go and look into the oil jars sitting in your cellar, and see what has become of his men."

Then, to his father's shock, Melisende strode over to the sideboard and poured herself a cup of wine. "The Seljuk army is gone, and on the morrow I start my journey home." She raised the cup high. "To your health, and, I hope, a long life, though I will not be here to save you next time." She drank the cup dry, then threw it on the floor and stormed out.

Mithra rose. "Father, we should see what is in the cellar."

"You believe this ill-mannered maid?" Ali Baba sputtered.

It took Mithra a moment to remember that what had sounded quite polite for Melisende, might not seem so to someone who hadn't heard how colourful her vocabulary could be. "Father, she has saved my life several times, and if she says that the Forty Thieves are here to seek vengeance, then I fear that not only is she telling the truth, but I have done her a grave discourtesy." Mithra led the way outside, not caring if his father followed.

The cellar still stank of corruption from Kasim's body, but it was stronger now, thick with the miasma of smoke and burned flesh. Mithra knew the stench of burning bodies, for he'd helped bring wood for more pyres than he cared to count.

"I don't know how, but we both owe her our lives. Forty times over, for the lives she has taken in our defence," Mithra said.

Father looked into one of the jars, then ran back up the cellar steps, retching.

Mithra followed him, his feet heavy with the new debt he now owed Melisende.

Only to find the lady herself, standing in the yard.

Mithra fell to his knees, then bowed until his forehead touched the dirt before her feet. "There is not enough gold in the world to repay you for the favour you have done for me, and for my family. Please, tell me how you accomplished this miracle."

She stared down at him for a long moment, then held out her hand to help him up. "Inside. Where I don't have to smell…all those cooked pigs."

Mithra could feel his father's eyes on him, but that didn't matter right now. All that mattered was Melisende.

He followed her back to the dining room, poured her a cup of wine, and waited for her to tell her tale.

Forty-Two

Her mouth was dry from talking so much, but she couldn't stop until she'd told it all. "I counted the corpses, realised there was one more man, perhaps the greatest danger of them all, so I came up to the house to find him. When I saw the dagger in his hand, I faltered for a moment, and that's when I spilled the sweets. Fortuitous, perhaps, because it gave me the opportunity to get close to him and do what needed to be done." Why was her cup dry? Surely she could not have drunk all that wine.

Mithra lifted the wine jug, and she shook her head. "Water," she said.

She drank and drank, but still she could taste the smoke and ash of burned bodies. It had seemed so clear at the time, but now horror washed over her at the thought of how many men she'd killed.

She could feel Ali Baba's eyes on her, watching everything. Whatever he thought of her, it could be no worse than what she thought of herself. Murderer of forty men...

Worse than that, why didn't she feel any guilt for what she'd done?

"It seems to me that we owe you everything. Our lives, our fortune...my son especially," Ali Baba began. "For such a debt, I can refuse you nothing. Anything you ask of me, I shall give you. Your freedom, wealth...anything."

"Father! Melisende is not a slave, and the wealth of the Forty Thieves properly belongs to her! You cannot offer her what is hers already!" Mithra protested.

Ali Baba bowed his head. "If my son, your most passionate defender, is correct, then I have little to offer. Except...my son himself, and my blessing upon your marriage. After all you have done, I would be honoured to accept you as a daughter."

Melisende stared at him. A moment ago, he'd been glowering at her for misbehaving, and now he was offering his son to her like some sort of prize.

Never mind that Mithra was a good man, the sort any girl would be happy to have as a husband. After that kiss the other day, Melisende could not deny she'd been entertaining thoughts of sharing his bed. Surely Ali Baba couldn't know about those thoughts…

Mithra's laughter cut through her reverie. "Father, that would be poor payment indeed! Lady Melisende is no maid, though she has pretended to be one for many weeks now, biding her time until she might go home. She is a Crusader lady, one who managed to escape from both the soldiers and the battle and hide in the forest, where I found her when I went out woodcutting. She saved me from the Forty Thieves, whose treasure trove I'd unwittingly stumbled upon, so I offered to help her hide until she might go home. That is her true heart's desire. She has no wish to be here with us. She wants to go home, and I propose to escort her there safely as soon as possible."

Ali Baba's face fell. "But what of your shop?"

Melisende almost laughed at his abrupt shift in focus. Men and their business – always, business came first.

"The shop is almost empty, with no goods left to sell. If this oil merchant had truly been what he said, then I might have had something, but as it is…I must travel to seek new goods I might trade, or return here to sell. Since Simon's death, I have been planning a trip to Rialto, and now is the time to take it. I shall take Lady Melisende with me, so that I may see her safely home."

Her heart sank. Home. The impossibly distant place she'd barely thought about in some time. She'd been so busy with her life here…

"We shall leave in three days," Mithra continued. "That should be long enough to bury the bodies, seek supplies for the journey, and to source suitable clothes for Lady Melisende."

Ali Baba nodded. "Yes, we must bury the bodies. If anyone knew what had happened here…no, they must not find out. The jars we can bury, too. But what of the horses?"

"We take them with us," Melisende said. "Two of them were born in my father's stables, and the rest will be able to carry goods or fetch a fine price in my homeland. You have a fortune in horseflesh in your stable. More than most men make in a lifetime."

But she'd have to go with him, to see that the horses sold at a proper price. Mithra didn't know horses the way she did.

Once she was home, she'd be happy again, Melisende told herself. She'd see everything she'd missed and wonder why she'd left in the first place. Dorylaeum, the crusade, murdering all those men…it would all seem like a fast-fading dream.

Yes, home was where she belonged. Not here.

She rose. "I shall retire. In the morning, we can begin our preparations for the journey."

Mithra rose too, then bowed deeply. "As my lady wishes."

His lady. A dream, and nothing more, she reminded herself, as she headed off to bed.

Forty-Three

Rialto was like another world, where the sea crept into the city, in aquamarine streets that Mithra had to remind himself he could not simply walk along.

For what felt like the thousandth time that day, he glanced at Melisende, who appeared to be as entranced as he was. He breathed a sigh of relief. Rialto was new to her, too, then. But his eyes lingered on her, on the layers of linen that looked just like his own clothes, as modest as anything she'd worn in Dorylaeum, and yet…

It was because she didn't wear a veil, he told himself, but that wasn't true. She hadn't covered her face in the house, or in the stables. Then again, she'd rarely smiled in Dorylaeum, but her lips seemed stuck in a permanent curve since they'd left. Her eyes lit up at the slightest thing, as she pointed to whatever had caught her interest to make sure he didn't miss it.

Melisende was the most delightful travelling companion a man could ever meet. If he hadn't fallen in love with her in Dorylaeum, he'd have done it again a dozen times over on the way to Rialto. It would break his heart when they parted.

But what else could they do? She was a highborn Crusader lady, headed home to her father and likely marriage to some Crusader lord. He was a merchant, newly risen to the position, who had yet to prove himself outside of the Dorylaeum market.

He would focus first on finding Simon's family, and giving them the gold that belonged to them. Perhaps then they would be willing to do business with him, or introduce him to other Rialto merchants who might.

A few enquiries about the Ziano family gave him the address of what he understood was the family patriarch's palace. It wasn't until he stood outside the grand edifice that put every single one of Dorylaeum's finest houses to shame that nerves began to knot in his belly. He was no one. He did not belong here. If he'd known how important Simon's family was, he would not have dared…

"Ooh, Duke Sebastiano Ziano's house! My brother said wonderful things about him when he came home from Rialto. I always hoped I'd get to meet him. What business do you have with him?" Melisende asked.

She'd insisted upon accompanying him, and Mithra hadn't had the heart to refuse her. She knew more than anyone where he'd come from, and how this was no place for a lowly woodcutter like him. But the Duke's servants might allow a Crusader lady inside…

Plenty of people crowded into the Duke's reception hall, yet the servant made the crowd part to allow them through. No, to let Lady Melisende through, Mithra reminded himself. He trailed behind her, carrying the pitifully small chest.

"Lady Melisende of Mareschal, and Master Mithra of Dorylaeum! Two people I never imagined I would get to meet, and yet, you are both here in my house!" The man who greeted them looked like a much older version of Simon, with an open smile that said he meant every word. "You must stay with me while you are here in Rialto. I insist upon it."

A few words to his servants, and he'd not only ordered refreshments for them, but guest rooms and instructions to bring their things from the ship.

Finally, the Duke gestured for them to sit as he took a seat for himself. "Lady Melisende, please forgive me if I seem insensitive to your beauty and the honour you do me in this visit, but your companion carries news of my brother that I have sorely craved for many months." The Duke's eyes turned to Mithra. "His letters are always full of news of you and his son, so I feel as if I know you, Master Mithra. My brother's last letter was full of his plans for returning to Rialto with his family, and leaving you to manage his business in

Dorylaeum as his partner. Yet here you are. Please, Master Mithra, what word do you bring of my brother Simon?"

The eagerness in the Duke's eyes smote Mithra's heart. That Simon had had such plans, plans he'd never shared with him, which might have saved Peter and all his family if he'd only left Dorylaeum sooner.

Haltingly, Mithra began, "Your Grace – "

"Sebastiano, please. Simon looked upon you like a son, which would make you near enough to my nephew."

Mithra nodded. His heart had never felt so heavy. Why, if he fell in the canal outside, his heart alone would drag him to the bottom of the sea. Yet he'd sworn to do this, and he owed it to Simon. "Simon, Peter, and all their family were killed by Seljuk soldiers. The army stormed Dorylaeum, slaughtered all the Christians, and claimed all their goods as their own. I was too late to save them, but I managed to keep the soldiers from looting the shop, and saved what I could from the warehouse. I asked myself what Master Simon would have done in my place, and I hope I was not wrong in opening his shop for business. I sold…everything, mostly to the soldiers themselves, and set the gold aside to return to his family when the Seljuk army had gone." He lifted the chest onto the Duke's desk and opened it so that the man might see the gold inside. It was a small chest, true, but it was full of gold coins. "I have since inherited my uncle's shop, and I had hoped to buy Simon's shop, too, now he has no use for it…" He stopped when he saw the Duke.

Sebastiano buried his face in his hands, openly weeping for the brother he'd lost. "It is as I feared! Simon should have left Dorylaeum long ago, I told him. But he would not listen. And now all that is left of him and his family is a cold box of coins." He closed the lid, and fastened it with a click. Then he pushed the box toward Mithra. "You are a good man, and an honest merchant, to have brought this here to me. But I am the Duke of Rialto, and you have come from a Seljuk city. I cannot accept any gifts from you, nor any gold. Nor can I trade with you, while your city and mine are at war. All I can offer you is what is lost to me –

everything my brother owned in Dorylaeum. His house, his shop, any goods that remained – they are yours now, just as Simon intended."

Mithra jumped to his feet. "But I cannot – "

The Duke held up his hand. "You must. For who else is more worthy of my brother's worldly goods than his only surviving son? I know you have a father, who I pray still lives, but one day, like Simon, you will wish to marry, and what if it goes against your father's wishes? Simon always followed his heart, like I did, and he would want you to do the same. With this gift, Simon would have set you free from all familial demands, and granted you the wealth to marry whatever girl you wished. I will gladly do what he could not."

Not whatever girl he wished, Mithra told himself, not daring to look at the woman beside him. The one who would always hold his heart.

Mithra mumbled his acceptance, and was greeted with a grateful smile from the Duke.

A moment later, Mithra was forgotten as the Duke turned to Melisende.

"What news of your brother?" he asked

eagerly.

"My brother?"

"Sir Godfrey, of course! You must have good news of his quest. Is that not why he has sent you?"

For the first time since he'd met Melisende, she did not seem to know what to say.

Forty-Four

"My brother was safe at home, the last time I saw him. I have not seen him since the Crusaders left our village. The last I heard, he was in Byzas. But that was months ago. Your Grace knows more about his movements than me, if you have seen him since then," Melisende said.

The Duke's face fell. "So he hasn't found my daughter yet?"

Godfrey had been searching for the killers of some girl he'd found, Melisende remembered. The Duke's daughter could not have been in her village at home. Could she?

"When did your daughter go missing, Your Grace? Was it before the Crusaders left?"

He shook his head. "No, some months after that. They'd already left Byzas, your brother said, when he kidnapped her."

No, Godfrey would never do such a thing! "You believe my brother kidnapped your daughter?" Unless this daughter was the reason he'd come home from Rialto in disgrace. There must be more to it, though…for Godfrey would never do something so dishonourable.

The Duke burst out laughing. "Lady Melisende, you and I both know Sir Godfrey would find it easier to fly than to kidnap a virtuous maiden. No, it was some rogue magician with his terrible arcane arts, he said, who stole my poor Penelope. Godfrey swore he'd go after them, and bring her back. Why would Godfrey steal her when your father and I wanted him to marry her? I won't deny your brother isn't the brightest lad, but he's not as stupid as that!"

Melisende breathed a sigh of relief. The dead girl wasn't the Duke's daughter, and her brother had evidently made amends for whatever crime he'd committed on his first trip to Rialto. While she had her doubts about her brother's ability to bring the girl back, if he found her at all, she didn't dare say so in front of the Duke. Instead, she said, "My brother may not have the sharpest wit, but what he lacks in quickness he makes up for with loyalty and honour and willingness to do whatever is necessary. If anyone can find Lady Penelope, it will be Sir Godfrey." Even if it took him twenty years, Melisende thought but did not say. "I hope she is soon returned to you, Your Grace."

"Yes." He stared at her for a moment, then clapped his hands. "But in her absence, you must join me for dinner. Both of you. I insist."

Before either of them could protest, Melisende and Mithra were herded off by the Duke's servants to a pair of adjacent and very opulent guest chambers, where suitable clothes had already been laid out.

Melisende stared at the gown, made of so much silk she'd rustle like a tree in a high wind at the slightest movement. There would be no running for her tonight.

"Would you like a hot bath, my lady?" a maid asked.

Melisende could not recall the last time she'd known such a luxury. "Oh yes," she said.

Forty-Five

Mithra arrived in the dining room to find only the Duke there. He felt a little less self-conscious in his borrowed finery when he realised the Duke was dressed almost the same.

They talked of small things at first, the weather and the way prices changed when one was at war, before the Duke moved to more serious matters, like when the war might end.

"Because I'm eager to get back to all the longstanding business arrangements in your city and those surrounding it. Wars are bad for business, as everyone knows. Once it's over, we can pick up where we left off, if that is amenable to you. Simon said you knew his business better than he did, and he had contacts everywhere. If I wanted silk, he had six men he could source it from, and another dozen if they did not arrive in time. Once this crusade is complete, you may expect the arrival of one of my sons, for I regret I am too old for such journeys myself." The Duke fell silent as his attention shifted elsewhere.

Mithra followed the man's gaze, and the vision that captivated his own gaze was brilliant enough to leave him gasping for breath.

"She's like an angel, isn't she? The Baron of Mareschal always was one to breed the most beautiful creatures, but he'd never part with one of the mares. I tried to get her for one of my sons – fair begged him, I did, but he'd hear none of it. Not even when I offered to marry her myself. Duchess of Rialto, highest lady in the land, was not good enough for little Lady Melisende. No amount of money would persuade her father to part with her. That's why I agreed to the marriage between his son and my daughter. If only the Seljuks and then the Crusaders hadn't ruined all our plans, eh, Master Mithra?"

But Mithra could not speak. He could only watch as Melisende floated into the room in a cloud of gold silk, which somehow showed every delicious curve of her body even as it covered it in the most modest way possible.

She wore a matching veil so gossamer thin that her hair caught the light through it, gleaming as she turned her head.

"My daughter Penelope made that dress. She wore it to a wedding once, and I think the only man with eyes for the poor bride was the groom! Seeing it on Lady Melisende makes me want to lock her away in the strongest room of the palace, with all the other priceless treasures, so no man could steal her. Do you not agree?"

Lock Melisende away? Mithra recoiled. No man who'd seen her face light up with every breath of wind, or shaft of sunlight, or watched her climb a tree, or run as though she would fly faster than the wind itself, or laugh as a bird alighted on the mast to eat a meal of fresh-caught fish…no man who'd seen her glorious soul shine out through her eyes could even think of committing such a crime against her.

Maybe Melisende's father was right to keep her away from such a man.

Melisende frowned and flicked at her skirt. For all its beauty, the gown restricted her steps, making her mince across the floor instead of the swift strides that came so naturally to her.

"No, Your Grace. All I want to do is set her free from everything that confines her."

The Duke stared at him for a moment, before he began to nod. "Ah, yes. You're a young man in your prime. Of course, bedding a naked angel like that would be bliss indeed."

Horrified that the Duke had taken his words in a way he had not meant them, Mithra opened his mouth to explain.

But Melisende was now close enough to touch, as well as hear every word, so he fell silent as she dropped a graceful curtsey.

Mithra's eyes nearly popped out of his skull as the slight tilt of her body let him see right down the front of her gown to the most perfect pair of breasts…

He closed his eyes. He would treasure that vision until his dying day.

"Your Grace, Master Mithra," she said. "Where is everyone else?"

Sebastiano beamed. "We are everyone, my dear. I have no desire to share you."

An angry sound came out of Mithra's throat before he could stop it.

The Duke added smoothly, "Except maybe with Master Mithra here, of course."

Melisende's smile sparkled like diamonds in the sun. Did he imagine it, or was she looking only at him?

"You must forgive Master Mithra if he is a little surprised to see me," she began. "For in Dorylaeum, you see, the women are not allowed to dine with the men."

"Dinners in Dorylaeum must be dull indeed, for I cannot imagine wishing to deny myself a moment with the beauty that is before me now," the Duke said.

How dare this old man try to seduce her!

"That is precisely the problem," Mithra said.

"You see, when a man is so beguiled by a woman's beauty, he may forget to eat or drink or speak to his companions at all. Now that is a dull dinner indeed!"

Melisende laughed merrily, but the Duke did not join in.

Forty-Six

By the end of the meal, Melisende could scarcely keep her eyes open. She had a vague idea that, as the highest ranking person there, the Duke had to dismiss them before she could retire to bed, but if he didn't do it soon, she was going to fall asleep on the table.

Finally, the Duke rose. "Lady Melisende, forgive me for keeping you up so late. It is rare that I have such fascinating company at dinner. You must allow me to take you for a tour of Rialto on the morrow."

Melisende bobbed a curtsey, not caring how

graceful it appeared as long as she didn't fall over. "Your Grace is too kind. Since Godfrey got home from Rialto, for months he talked about the beauty of the churches here, and the exquisite artwork. I confess I have been terribly envious of him for quite some time."

The Duke bowed. "Then on the morrow, your envy will be at an end. And tonight, should you wish to confess and absolve yourself of such a terrible sin, I will see that the priest in my private chapel is available to you."

She opened her mouth to protest, then closed it again as she realised it had been many months since her last confession, and she would be wise to accept the Duke's generous offer. So she muttered something she hoped sounded grateful, and headed up to her room.

She found Mithra a step behind her. Oh, of course – his room was beside hers.

"May I speak to you for a moment?" he asked. "Privately?"

"Of course," she said, following him into his room.

His bed was enormous – just like hers – and

seemed to dominate the room. It would definitely dominate her dreams tonight, too, for Mithra was never far from her thoughts.

Melisende chose a chair as far from the bed as possible. "What do you wish to discuss?" she asked.

"What do you intend to confess?" he demanded.

She stared at him. He was not a Christian, but he'd lived with one, so surely he knew about the sanctity of the confessional. Though it was possible that he did not…

"My deepest, darkest secrets, so that I may be forgiven," she said.

Mithra shook his head. "You cannot tell this priest about the Forty Thieves, or their cave, or what happened to them. If anyone were to find out, they would arrest us both and kill us for our crimes!"

"What can I tell him, then?" Melisende demanded.

"Maybe that you ran off on a crusade. Surely you regret running away from your family."

She thought for a moment, longer and harder than she thought she'd need to, but still the answer was the same. "I do not regret it for a moment. The church encouraged this crusade, so the priest would praise me for it, instead of calling it a sin. And I am of age, entitled to run away from my family if and when I desire. Perhaps not wise to do so, but I did it, and I refuse to regret it."

"There must be something!"

There was, and she would probably regret saying it aloud, but it would serve him right for being so obstinate about this. She could confess to whatever she pleased, and no man could stop her.

She rose and met his gaze. "Yes. For some weeks now, I have regretted one thing. Not the crusade, not my time in Dorylaeum, and not any of the things I did there. Except the night the Forty Thieves came."

"You cannot tell him – "

"I don't regret killing them. They were criminals, and I did what was right to protect the man I loved. Maybe if I were a better, kinder person, I would feel guilt for the lives I ended. But the truth is that I did not. I still don't. If you had seen the things they'd done…" Melisende took a deep breath. "I regret that I did not tell your father the truth that night. When he offered me anything I desired, and you said you would take me home…I wish I'd had the courage to say what I wanted. Whether it could be mine or not. I regret not saying what was in my heart."

She looked up to find Mithra staring at her. He'd done that plenty over dinner, but this time it was different.

He stepped forward and grasped her hands. "My father's debt is mine as much as his. Anything you want, if it is within my power, I would give it to you. You have but to name it, Lady Melisende, and it is yours."

She didn't want to look at him, and yet she could not tear her eyes away. Tears blurred her vision. "You. I wanted…for one brilliant moment, I wanted to marry you."

"But I am a lowly woodcutter, a man your father would scarcely notice. You've had marriage offers from dukes that he's refused. He would never agree to let me marry you."

"My father can go play hide the sausage with the Duke…or the devil himself, if he desires, but I'll have none of them. In Dorylaeum, it might be different, but here I am of age, which makes me the mistress of my own destiny. If I wish to marry a penniless young woodcutter, I will. Or if I want to marry a good, kind, wonderful man, whose first thought when he stumbles across a priceless treasure is to help other people, whose kisses burn hotter than the desert sands in the sun…then I would damn anyone to hell who dares to object." Then the fire in her died at the thought of the one man who might object, as he had that night, and silence her on this matter forever.

"Melisende…"

He was going to tell her he didn't love her, wasn't he? It would break her heart, but she would bear it. She must bear it. At least she'd found the courage to confess her feelings to him. To know he did not share them…

"How do weddings among your people work?"

When she looked up, startled, to meet his eyes again, he continued, "You see, it's simple back home. The couple simply sleep together for a night under the same roof, and they're considered married. Seda is now considered my father's second wife, seeing as she lives with him, even though he only shares a bed with my mother. So if it's just a matter of sharing my bed, I'd happily take you as my wife tonight."

Her mouth was dry. Why was her mouth so dry? That burning look in his eyes. It seemed to set some sort of fire inside her. The very thought of his hands, his lips on her skin…

"The bedding…that bit comes after the wedding," she managed to say. "The wedding is where we make promises in front of a priest."

The idea seemed to come to them both at once.

"The Duke said there was a priest at your service in his private chapel. Do you think…?"

Melisende grabbed his hand and strode toward the chapel.

Forty-Seven

Promises said in front of a priest took almost no time at all, and then Mithra had Melisende back in his chamber. By her people's customs, she was his wife. But by his, she would not be truly his wife until she'd cried out his name in joy.

Right. Now was not the time to tell her he'd never bedded a woman before.

There were a thousand and one ways to pleasure a woman, he told himself. If he could remember merely a few of them, it would be enough.

He prayed he would be enough.

Melisende stood staring at the bed with her back to him, her silk gown glimmering in the candlelight. No cave of treasure had ever tempted him half as much as she did right now.

He stepped up behind her, pressing her body against his, as he bent his head to kiss her throat. His fingers worked on the lacings that bound her gown so tightly about her body. On each side, and again at the back.

She shivered in his arms.

"You have no need to fear me, Melisende. I swear, I will never hurt you. Whatever those soldiers did to you, I will not."

She twisted in his arms, so that she faced him. "No soldier has ever touched me. You're the only man who has, and we stopped before you could..." She blushed.

"You're a virgin still?" He scarcely believed it.

Wordlessly, she nodded.

Untouched. How had he not guessed?

"I promise I will never hurt you."

He'd have to be so careful. But with

someone so precious, how could he not be?

He would start slow.

Carefully, Mithra leaned in for a kiss.

Oh, but he'd forgotten how one kiss with her could set the world on fire.

"Mithra, oh my God, Mithra!"

He blinked. As if this was their first kiss all over again, somehow he'd backed her up against the wall, with her legs up around his waist, but this time, his fingers were inside her, circling and stroking as her irresistible heat contracted around them.

She threw her head back and screamed his name again.

"You said you'd take me to bed after three times. That's seven, Mithra. Please!" she begged.

Seven. He'd pleasured her seven times already? Only…nine hundred and ninety-four to go.

He undid the final set of lacings, and gold silk slid down her body to puddle on the floor. The next layer was white silk, laced up the front so tightly that her breasts seemed ready to burst out the top. He gave the hem of her shift the slightest tug, and two perfect pink nipples peeked out.

All the ways he could pleasure her by caressing her breasts popped into his mind. He longed to try them all. But he wanted to take her to bed, too…

"Three more," he said, touching his tongue to one of those exquisite pink pearls.

Forty-Eight

Naked as her name day, her heart still thrumming in her chest from the blindingly perfect pleasure her husband had already given her, more times than she could count, Melisende knew she could not put off that fateful moment any longer. If she did, her courage might fail her.

So she lay down on the bed, propped up by an obscene number of pillows, and said, "Please, Mithra, make me your wife." Then she closed her eyes and prayed he would be swift, like her sisters in law had told her their first times had been.

She heard the swish of fabric – Mithra undressing, she had no doubt – and considered peeking, but the ladies had advised against it. If her husband was large, the sight of him would likely frighten her, and if he was small…well, men were sensitive about their man parts, so she'd been warned not to say anything about them at all.

She felt the pillows beside her shift as her husband's weight settled upon them, instead of on her, as she expected.

Strong hands seized her, lifting her as easily as if she were one of the feather pillows and not a flesh and blood woman. He set her down on his lap, straddling him as though he expected her to ride him like some sort of horse. But the heat of him between her thighs was like no horse. It made her yearn to feel his touch there again, a mixture of hardness and heat that almost made her swoon.

She grabbed his shoulders to steady herself, her hands closing on even more hot, hard flesh.

Melisende's eyes flew open, and for the first

time she saw her husband naked. His arms, shoulders and chest were just as muscular as she remembered, when she'd pushed him up against that tree. She wanted to run her hands along every ridge, touch her tongue to every dimple, to kiss…

He wore nothing but a lazy grin as he met her gaze. "I know not what you've heard about Crusader husbands, but marriage among my people is a very different thing. It is up to a wife to take a husband, and if I do not please you, you can divorce me by simply saying so. So, will you take me, Lady Melisende, and wed your body to mine?" His fingers stole between her legs again, stroking slowly.

She opened for him, like a flower who could not resist the sun. "Yes, oh, yes."

And then he glided into her, burning her with the most glorious heat, as his hands closed around her hips once more and ground her against him.

Her sisters in law had talked of pain, but Melisende felt nothing but pleasure and the burning desire for more.

"Oh, God, yes!" she cried. "Oh my God,

Mithra, do that again!"

Within moments, they found a rhythm, their bodies rising and falling as one, until waves of pleasure rolled over Melisende and she screamed for joy at the top of her lungs. And again, and again, and again, until they lay together, spent.

"Do I please you, Lady Melisende?" Mithra asked as he stroked her breasts.

She wanted him to take one of her nipples in his mouth, and do that thing with his tongue…

"Oh my God, yes!" Melisende said.

"Well enough to be allowed to share your bed for another night?"

"Every night for the rest of my life. And every day, too," she said dreamily.

Mithra chuckled. "Good. For there are a thousand and one ways to pleasure a woman, and I don't think I've tried more than a dozen so far. If I have my wish, I intend to spend each and every night showing you all the ways I remember. Should I forget any, I know I shall have you to remind me, for it is my hope that every night we share shall be branded into your memory, as every moment we have spent together already is branded into mine. You have saved my life and my family and my fortune. Now you hold my heart, and I will spend the rest of my life showing you how grateful I am for it."

She wanted to reply with equal eloquence, but he touched his tongue to her nipple and all coherent words left her with only a rapturous moan in response.

Some hours later, after they'd made love for the third time and her joyous screams had likely woken half the city, she laid her head on his chest and said sleepily, "When we return home to Dorylaeum, I want you to buy me as big a bed as this one, where we can make love every night."

"And every morning," he replied, wrapping his arms around her.

She lifted her head, eyes widening. "We can do it again in the morning?"

"I understand it is the sweetest way to start the day."

"Wake me at dawn, then, so we can find out together." Her eyes drifted shut.

"I will."

About the Author

Demelza Carlton has always loved the ocean, but on her first snorkelling trip she found she was afraid of fish.

She has since swum with sea lions, sharks and sea cucumbers and stood on spray drenched cliffs over a seething sea as a seven-metre cyclonic swell surged in, shattering a shipwreck below.

Demelza now lives in Perth, Western Australia, the shark attack capital of the world.

The *Ocean's Gift* series was her first foray into fiction, followed by her suspense thriller *Nightmares* trilogy. She swears the *Mel Goes to Hell* series ambushed her on a crowded train and wouldn't leave her alone.

Want to know more? You can follow Demelza on Facebook, Twitter, YouTube or her website, Demelza Carlton's Place at:

www.demelzacarlton.com

Books by Demelza Carlton

Siren of Secrets series

Ocean's Secret (#1)
Ocean's Gift (#2)
Ocean's Infiltrator (#3

Siren of War series

Ocean's Justice (#1)
Ocean's Widow (#2)
Ocean's Bride (#3)
Ocean's Rise (#4)
Ocean's War (#5)
How To Catch Crabs

Nightmares Trilogy

Nightmares of Caitlin Lockyer (#1)
Necessary Evil of Nathan Miller (#2)
Afterlife of Alana Miller (#3)

Mel Goes to Hell series

The Devil's Work (#1)
See You in Hell (#2)
Mel Goes to Hell (#3)
To Hell and Back (#4)
The Holiday From Hell (#5)
All Hell Breaks Loose (#6)
The Devil Goes to Heaven (#7)

Romance Island Resort series

Maid for the Rock Star (#1)
The Rock Star's Email Order Bride (#2)
The Rock Star's Virginity (#3)
The Rock Star and the Billionaire (#4)
The Rock Star Wants A Wife (#5)
The Rock Star's Wedding (#6)
Maid for the South Pole (#7)

Romance a Medieval Fairytale series

Enchant: Beauty and the Beast Retold
Dance: Cinderella Retold
Fly: Goose Girl Retold
Revel: Twelve Dancing Princesses Retold
Silence: Little Mermaid Retold
Awaken: Sleeping Beauty Retold
Embellish: Brave Little Tailor Retold
Appease: Princess and the Pea Retold
Blow: Three Little Pigs Retold
Return: Hansel and Gretel Retold
Wish: Aladdin Retold
Melt: Snow Queen Retold
Spin: Rumpelstiltskin Retold
Kiss: Frog Prince Retold
Reflect: Snow White Retold
Roar: Goldilocks Retold
Cobble: Elves and the Shoemaker Retold
Float: Enchanted Horse Retold
Steal: Forty Thieves Retold
Call: Pied Piper Retold